A FORMER MARI[NE'S]
PERSONAL WAR A[GAINST]
AND HUMAN TR[AFFICKERS IN THE]
SOUTHERN CALIFORNIA DESERT.

Drew, a former Marine sniper, his partner, and an unemployed slacker become entangled in a human-trafficking ring. After a devastating financial setback, Drew reluctantly agrees to transport human cargo. Hired on to transport "special cargo," their only instructions are not to inspect the load. The discovery they make places them in the crosshairs of a sadistic cartel leader. In the desert, they join forces with an-on-the run narcotics detective and former cartel *sicario*. What follows is a dangerous cat-and-mouse game to save the cargo and themselves through the back-country desert of Southern California. The desert holds a path for a new life or death for all those attempting the dangerous crossing.

The Silence and the Dark is a no nonsense, go for the jugular thrill ride, yet nuanced with heart felt emotions and plenty of surprises! One of the best debuts I've read in a very long time. I can't wait to read Marc Carlos' next effort! —*Matt Coyle, Author of the bestselling Anthony Award-winning Rick Cahill crime novels*

An excellent and poignant novel. The author describes each scene so vividly the readers are transported as if they were actually there. A gut-wrenching story that moves quickly and keeps the reader engaged. While this story is fictional, it could just as well be an expose on today's immigration plight. A must read for anyone who enjoys a suspense filled action novel. —*Merle Norman, Author of Finders Keepers*

i

"No disrespect, *amigos, pero,* you have seen me. There is no turning back on this now. Not a question of being in or not. You are all," Caritas was looking directly at Drew, "most definitely in."

"We know where you live," Fatty couldn't help himself. "We know what your kids look like."

The muscles and tendons in Drew's forearms twitched, firing with violence that begged to be unleashed.

"*No se preocupen,* don't worry, boys," Caritas said as he swept the wallets and other items off the hood of the Escalade and onto the dirt. The dust cloud was still swirling as Caritas walked toward Drew and Chino.

"Do the job. Don't fuck around. Get paid. *Muy simple, que no?*"

THE SILENCE AND THE DARK

Marc X. Carlos

Moonshine Cove Publishing, LLC
Abbeville, South Carolina U.S.A.
First Moonshine Cove edition June 2019

ISBN: 978-1-945181-603
Library of Congress PCN: 2019941805
Copyright 2019 by Marc X. Carlos

Cover image used with permission of the author, cover and interior design by Moonshine Cove staff.

Acknowledgment

Special thanks to my wife, Tonya, for listening to the story and encouraging me to put it down on paper. I could not have done it without her. To my daughter, Siena, for trudging through a rough first draft and for her ideas. Charles Rees for his help in tightening up the story. To my dad, a lifelong non-fiction reader, who actually enjoyed the novel. Also, much praise for John Cannon at JCannon Books for the initial editing and keeping the story honest, Drew thanks you. Finally, while this novel is a work of fiction, the reality of the dangers at the border and the human tragedy of hundreds of thousands of men, women and children seeking a better life remains a daily truth.

Dedication

For Pops

THE SILENCE

AND THE

DARK

ONE

He needed the money. There was no other way. Driving in his rattling truck, gas gauge already in the red, Drew wondered if his wife would forgive him if things didn't work out. He kept looking into his rearview mirror, just below the photo of his two boys stuffed in the cracked sun visor, and wondered why he was so nervous. After all, he hadn't done anything . . . yet.

Maybe Chino had a better idea this time. Well, he thought, at least a plan of some sort. He knew it wouldn't be a well-thought-out plan but, at the very least, he hoped it would have a real beginning and not a dangerous end. Whatever it was, he knew it wasn't something on the books. He wasn't going to need references.

"I know this guy who can get us in on this thing," Chino told him, not wanting to elaborate on the phone.

A guy and a thing. The beginning of every hard-luck story in America. Drew knew that, but he still found himself driving on this scorched desert road to hear about the "thing."

Time was running out for Drew. He knew it. He could feel the pressure every day. The savings from his Marine Corps service were running out. Back here in the world, particularly in the la-la land of Southern California, there were no jobs for trained killers. Previous job experience: travel to Middle Eastern countries, meet new people, shoot them dead. "Sniper" has no transferable job skills and tends to creep out employers. The crash of the economy sure did not help, and he found himself competing for jobs twenty or thirty deep with applicants. Explaining that your best skill is lowering your resting heart rate to thirty-nine beats per minute so you can gently squeeze a trigger and kill someone does not help your Home Depot application.

Pulling into the diner off the two-lane highway outside of Calipatria in scorching Imperial County, Drew could see Chino's faded blue F-150 backed into a spot out front, as if he were thinking he needed to make a quick getaway. Four trucks in the parking lot, a rusted newspaper rack in the front, and an old, faded sign that read "Mickey's" did not necessarily scream danger as much as flat-out depression. He pulled his truck into a marked spot and sat for a long minute. The temperature gauge on his dashboard read 116 degrees. He thought he should just turn around and head back to San Diego. Looking up again at the creased photo of little Drew and Jake, pure tow-headed six- and eight-year-old innocence, he knew that if things went wrong, their lives would change forever. Then again, if he didn't do something soon to change his situation, everything he had worked for and his family's future would be gone.

Fuck it. Drew took a deep breath and slowly let it out. The still running air conditioner cooled his body. He turned the engine off, looked up the photo again and flipped the visor up. He opened the door, and the hot sun immediately assaulted him. Drew squinted into the laser brightness and reached into the truck to pull out his Chargers ball cap. He put the cap on and pulled the bill low to shield his eyes. As he made his way toward the entrance, Drew looked through the large glass window and saw only a few people eating in two of the red vinyl booths. Once inside, Drew spotted him in a booth at the far end. Chino was sitting with his back to the wall. Although he was wearing his one of his endless supply of San Diego Padres T-shirts, Chino's blunt-cut hair made no attempt to hide his military background. Drew always thought the buzzed hair on top of Chino's wide head made it look like his scalp was about to blow off. He used to joke that he looked like the Mexican Incredible Hulk. Chino was tearing through a chorizo burrito, red grease stains on his fingers and mouth.

Christ, he thought, with all the shit that might happen to them, Chino was shoving food down his face like it was a normal day in the life of an unemployed, Chinese-Mexican former Marine. As he got to the table, Drew noticed a plate with half-eaten huevos rancheros and a steaming cup of coffee.

Chino looked up from his burrito mess.

"What up, Drew," he said with a head nod and a smile.

"Who are you here with?" Drew said as he looked at the other plate.

"Oh," Chino wiped his mouth with a wadded-up napkin, "he's my boy, the guy I was telling you about."

Drew trusted Chino with his life. Chino always had his back, both in Iraq and Afghanistan. Chino was his insurance, his armor. This guy was not something they had talked about for this meeting.

"What the fuck, Chino?"

"Don't trip, man." Chino was eyeing the rest of his burrito slopped in the plate and was debating whether to pick it up and finish the assault. "Dude is cool, I worked with him before the Corps."

"At fucking Walmart?"

"Well," he said, now thinking better and pushing the plate away, "yeah, but . . ."

Chino stopped midsentence and looked over at his friend now walking back from the restroom. Drew turned and gave him the judgmental once over. He was short, overweight and dressed like some rapper wanna-be—XXXL Lakers tank over an XXL white T-shirt, complete with a wide, stiff brim Lakers ball cap cocked sideways with his ears tucked inside. The fade and manicured chin strap facial hair did not help his appearance. Basically, a fat white guy in clown clothes.

Jesus, Drew thought, *I hate this guy already.*

"'Sup, dude?" the guy said, looking first to Chino then to Drew.

"Drew, this is my boy Chance."

Chance threw out his meaty fist for a bump that did not come his way. Drew looked him up and down one more time.

"Chino," Drew said as he leaned back against the squeaky vinyl bench seat, "I don't know this guy and . . ."

"Check it out, Drew." Chino practically pleaded. "Just listen to what he has to say, you don't like it, we walk away. Cool?"

Drew did not respond. Instead, he turned and looked back over his shoulder at the nearly empty diner. Eight booths with the same cracked red vinyl seating, a row of flickering fluorescent lights that made the grey counters and floors look old and tired. This is what it has come to, he thought. He saw no other choice. He slumped lower into his seat.

TWO

It was strange to Gerardo that it was not as dark as he expected. The night sky was without clouds, and the stars seemed to occupy every inch. The half-moon illuminated the narrow trail, and the only other light came from a group leader's small flashlight. Looking up, Gerardo couldn't help but wonder if the same sky loomed over his hometown. He followed the ragtag collection of twenty or so men and women down a twisted, gravely path into the desert.

"*Andale!*? one of the leaders yelled back to the straggling group.

"*Estoy cansada,*" said an old woman who gasped for breath. "Can we take a rest?"

The man walked back toward her and yanked her up by the makeshift bed sheet pack on her back.

"No, *vieja,*" he said, forcibly straightening her. "We need to get out of this shit while it is still dark to reach the pickup point. You don't keep up, we leave you behind."

Gerardo wanted to help, but he needed to focus on his own problems, which, at present, were getting through this desert and out of Mexico. Everyone out here had a family to get back to, a wife, a child. They were all hard stories. Gerardo had no time to care about them.

The group started to move again. Looking around as he descended the steep trail, he noticed two children, a boy and a girl no more than six or seven years old, quietly navigating the path. He had been walking now for more than an hour and had not even noticed them. He saw an additional ten or so children strung out behind them.

Gerardo made eye contact with the little boy. The boy didn't say a word. Under the moonlit sky, the whites of the boy's eyes stood out. Gerardo noticed the boy was holding onto a rope, and he was tied at the waist to the little girl. The boy looked up at Gerardo and then turned back to the little girl and tugged on the rope, urging her to move forward.

Gerardo knew this was not normal, but he did his best to keep it out of his thoughts. *Not my life,* he thought, *not my problem.* He looked up at the stars again and wondered if they were in America yet. Out here everything looked the same. Funny how that was. It might look the same, but just a shift in the border made it an entirely new world. The same stars, the same dirt. The difference was that people were willing to die to be here.

THREE

"It's all about the *pollos*, Drew."

"The what?"

"The wetbacks, the mezkins," Chance said.

Drew lowered the brim of his ball cap as if to emphasize secrecy in the near-empty diner. Drew really did not like this guy. He really didn't like him any better after calling Mexicans wetbacks, given that his mother was first-generation Mexican-American. His father had raised him never to make disparaging remarks about other people because of where they were from. Then again, his father did not raise him to be a criminal.

"Yeah, Drew, it's the new drug . . ." Chino pushed his plate away, "this isn't some dangerous cocaine or meth run."

"Look, it's real easy," Chance looked around again and lowered his voice. "I know a dude who needs guys like us."

"Like us?" Drew could not believe that this pathetic blob could consider himself to be in the same league. One tour in Iraq. One in Afghanistan. This guy in the electronics sections of Walmart with a bright red name tag.

"We just need to transport and keep the peace amongst the wetbacks," Chance nearly whispered.

"Our job is to run them from Ocotillo, or some other spot in the desert, to North County, just short of the checkpoint.?" Chino pinched up chorizo remnants off his plate with a piece of tortilla.

The checkpoint at San Clemente was an on-again, off-again border checkpoint that served as a dividing line between San Diego County and Orange County. Once past the checkpoint, an undocumented crosser could easily make it to Los Angeles or further north without fear of being caught.

"We run three vehicles, six or eight illegals per vehicle. Run the back-mountain roads, maybe a little off-road sometimes. Three times a week." Chance leaned back with his fat hands extended upward. "Easy money, baby!"

Of course, Drew knew better. He knew involvement with this idiot would lead to disaster. He also knew he would regret his decision to sit down in the booth instead of walking away. He knew all of this, but he was out of options.

"What about the money?" The words came out easier than Drew had expected.

"Still working on that, but I'm pretty sure it is in the hundreds per head each run . . . cash!" Somehow Chance made the word sound dirty.

"Look Drew," Chino placed his hand on Drew's shoulder, "we could both use this. Things are pretty tough out there for both of us."

That was putting it lightly.

FOUR

The trail leveled off after descending into low shrubs and rocky, flat terrain. The mountains were behind them, and intermittent lights of passing cars were visible miles ahead of them. The landscape, stark with waist-high mesquite and jagged rock, had a desperate feel to it. Gerardo felt like he was part of a desperate group. The young and old focused only on getting out of the desert and into some type of safe house, even though many knew they would be packed in a windowless structure to await transportation to a final destination. From there they could connect with family members and return to or seek out life-crushing manual labor for which most Americans would not even get out of bed. The lucky ones got jobs as fast-food workers, hotel housekeepers, or nannies. They were the ones who dissolved into the landscape. The dishwashers in the fancy bistros, the workers at the carwash, the nameless men blowing leaves and debris from one property to another. All of this low-wage toiling was better than slaving for a few pesos a week and dealing with daily cartel violence.

As they passed through a veritable forest of yucca and high boulders, the leader of the group came to an abrupt stop.

"*Alto! Juntos todos!*" the guide called as he signaled with his arm that they should assemble in the cover of rocks and cacti. After walking for more than three hours, it felt good to sit and rest in the dirt. While the guides were speaking in low tones on their cellphones, Gerardo was able to make out the faces of some of the others around him as they sat in a loose circle under the moonlight. The group was larger than he had originally thought. There were probably twenty-five total. Although he had never crossed before, it seemed strange to him that the group included at least ten children. The children looked to be under ten years old, and they were attached in pairs by rope around their waists. None of the children seemed to have parents or family members with them. The other adults in the group turned their backs to the children in what appeared to be a conscious effort not to look at them.

Gerardo noticed that the guides had their backs to him. He made eye contact with the boy he had seen earlier.

"*Chamacito*," Gerardo whispered to get his attention.

"How are you and your sister doing?"

The little boy, still as a statue, could not have been more than eight. He had a thick and unruly mop of dark hair. The Bart Simpson T-shirt he was wearing said "Ay, Caramba!" and looked to be about two sizes too big. The little girl attached to him looked to be about the same age. She was dressed in a frayed dark dress with her hair pulled back in a ponytail. She looked over at Gerardo, said nothing and then looked away.

"*No es mi hermana*," the boy responded, looking over to the guides.

"*Es tú prima?*" Gerardo asked, aiming to put him at ease by asking if the girl was his cousin.

The boy replied that he did not know her. He quickly returned his gaze to the ground ahead of him, but Gerardo could see the boy cast his gaze left at the smugglers.

"Where are your parents?" Gerardo asked in Spanish.

The boy did not answer. The blank stare he gave to Gerardo made it clear that he had none.

The guides who had been outside the perimeter returned, and one of them ordered everyone to stand.

"Another half hour to our pickup spot. Everyone keep moving." The guide, wearing a Dallas Cowboys jersey, could not have been older than eighteen.

Gerardo tried to maintain focus on the trail, but questions invaded his thoughts. He was paying almost one thousand dollars to cross. How could these children afford to cross? Why did not any family members come with them? Part of him already knew the answer to the most troubling question—where they were going. He looked back as they began to walk and could clearly see there were, in fact, twelve children. Six girls and six boys. They were paired up and tied at the waist, and a long rope connected the entire group to one of the guides. To Gerardo, they looked like little prisoners of war.

FIVE

Drew enlisted in the Marine Corps after watching a CNN report about a terrorist attack on an embassy post in the Middle East. He had come from a family of tried-and-true American dreamers. The dream that America was the best at everything. The best lifestyles, the best movies, the best government, the best sports. He grew up listening to his father and his uncles rant about communism and socialism and the general degradation of the American way of life. God was on our side, his father used to say. NASCAR, monster trucks, and NFL football were religion to his family.

All of this was coursing through his mind as he drove his truck up the mountain grade on Interstate 8 toward San Diego. The remoteness of the landscape, boulder-pocked hillsides, and clay-colored dirt reminded Drew of photos he had seen of Mars watching Nat Geo with the boys. Plenty of time to think.

Drew was acutely aware of the ironic collision of his beliefs and what he agreed to do. He did his best to justify it. Like a firefight, he thought, you get backed up, and you fight your way out. The nagging truth for Drew was that while his circumstances seemed dire, it was not life or death. But Drew felt the crushing weight of it all. The fear of losing it all. If he lost the house he bought for his young family, then he would lose the dignity he had fought so hard to maintain after his release from the military. How could his wife, a daughter of privilege, stay with him? How could his children respect him?

Looking off to the dirt roads and fire trails that spanned the desert, Drew wondered if he would be transporting illegal border crossers along the same roads. The thought of people, including children, traversing the Martian terrain on foot seemed impossible. On this winding highway, there was plenty of time to think. He kept telling himself these were just hardworking, family types he would be bringing across. Still, he knew he could just as well be transporting terrorists, gang members, or killers.

There was still another hour on the road until he reached San Diego. Plenty of time to think. Plenty of time to rationalize. Plenty of time to worry.

SIX

Not my problem, Gerardo did his best to convince himself. Wherever these kids were going was not his problem. His problem was getting out of Sinaloa, out of Mexico, out of the life that would inevitably lead to his death. He told himself he could fade into the background here in the United States. Be just like any other immigrant. Work hard, save some money. Maybe a few beers on Saturday night, find a woman. Maybe . . .

Part of him couldn't leave it alone. Every time he looked away, he felt his gaze pulled back to the children. Looking at them tied together two by two, he couldn't help but remember the illustrated Bible he had as a kid. The scene looked like the animals being led to Noah's Ark. Gerardo had been to border towns in the past. He had seen people preparing for "the crossing". Old women, men. Women with babies. Children carrying babies. This, however, was like nothing he had ever seen.

Gerardo snapped the thought out of his mind. He kept his eyes low beneath the brim of his ball cap so the guides would not see his eyes wandering toward the children. He noticed that while there were about twenty or so adults in his group, only one armed guide walked alongside them. The children had four guides with them. Two in the front. Two in the back.

Gerardo could feel the gaze of the smuggler beside him, so he cast his eyes down toward the dirt trail. He trudged silently along under the star-filled sky along with other faceless cargo. Not my problem. Not my problem.

He kept trying to convince himself, but it was not working.

SEVEN

She knew what she was getting into with a man like Drew. Growing up in La Jolla meant the Beach & Tennis Club and private schools. Charity League balls and over-the-top sweet-sixteen parties. Everyone she knew from high school had gone off to universities and graduated. Some had Wall Street jobs; others were lawyers or teachers. Katie had stayed close to home. Two uninspired years at San Diego State had left her drifting without a compass. Katie was frustrated because she found the men she dated were just boys. None had any drive, any plans. Chargers games, fish tacos, and day drinking in Pacific Beach bars summed up her existence until she met Drew.

It was just a night with no plans until a friend persuaded her to go to a country-western bar. Right, Katie thought, a bunch of shit-kicking hicks in boots, cowboy hats, and ridiculous belt buckles. Maybe they could invent a drinking game based on the number of Wrangler jeans they counted. But as the thought of country bar silliness crossed her mind, she considered the alternative. An evening of the same old thing. Surfers and wanna-be's in sagging, unwashed jeans, T-shirts and ball caps with surf logos.

What the heck, cowboys couldn't be any worse.

That night she and two friends walked into The Two Step and felt like they were touring a cheap roadside museum in Texas. The gawking the girls were doing was only slightly less obvious than pointing fingers at people. True to form, there were big belt buckles and cowboy hats. Everyone, men and women, was wearing western boots. The loud beat and twangy reverb of country music were on a nonstop loop. She knew the people on the dance floor were line dancing, but she had no idea how or where it started or ended.

The trio sidled up to a corner of the enormous bar to order drinks, and in seconds flat men descended upon them. While Katie's friends found it exciting to be the center of attention, Katie felt the crushing regret of an intruder. The men who surrounded them all looked the same. They spoke in some sort of strained country drawl. It was hard to believe they were only fifteen miles from the beach.

The blaring country music and the clamoring of the fake cowboys competing for attention from the girls became too much for Katie.

"I'll be right back," she told one of her friends.

Katie walked toward an empty space at the far end of the bar and asked the bartender for a club soda. Catching a glimpse of herself in the bar mirror, she could sense she did not belong here. Her long blonde hair was natural and free, not over-dyed and blown out. Her blue eyes had only a light liner to them instead of the paint mural background of most of the girls in the bar. Feeling like a loner, she did what any loner in a bar does, she took out her phone and began to scroll down her media pretending to be busy or important. Katie sat sideways to the bar, hunched over the phone on her lap.

"How's the field trip, ma'am?"

The voice came from over her right shoulder. She gave a half turn of her head.

"Excuse me?" she asked.

Leaning against the bar stood what seemed to be the only man in the bar not cowboyed up. He was about six-two, wearing regular fitting jeans and a simple black T-shirt. No cowboy hat, no trucker hat, no ridiculous belt buckle. Everything about him exuded confidence and ease that Katie was not used to seeing in men in her circles. Clean shaven, straight teeth with a disarming smile that made her want to stay put and talk to him. He was well built, although he didn't try to show it off in a too-tight shirt. His hair was cut short and razor clipped. Katie had grown up in this military town and was accustomed to seeing soldiers in uniforms and civilian clothes. The Marines were in North County at Camp Pendleton. The Navy was in Coronado and at Thirty-Second Street. Anybody who grew up in San Diego could spot a military man from a mile away. By the looks of his cut, he was definitely a Marine.

"You and your friends look like you are doing research for some school project," he said.

Katie was about to act offended until he smiled again. A simple, friendly smile. The type of smile that could diffuse a tense situation. The type of smile that made you forget what you were mad about. Not forced, completely natural.

The type of smile that made women not want to be with anyone else.

"Is it that obvious?" she asked with a shrug of her shoulders.

"Pretty much, ma'am."

"Do you always call women your age ma'am?"

"Yes, ma'am," he shifted his stance with hands stuffed in his front pockets, "Unless I get to know them well. Then I call them something else."

"And what is that?" Katie couldn't help but ask.

"Darlin'," he said with a smile.

Katie laughed. Is this guy for real?

"Well," Katie was beaming, "to tell you the truth, I like darlin' better than ma'am."

"So do I, darlin'."

Katie couldn't look away from the unwavering blue-gray eyes.

"What's your name, cowboy?"

"Drew. You can call me Drew."

Katie laughed. "You can call me Katie, but right now, I'm kind of liking darlin'."

EIGHT

Drew drove his truck up the long gravel driveway of the 1960s ranch-style house that he and Katie purchased just before the housing market crashed. The house needed work when they bought it. The paint was cracking and flaking at the corners. The shutters on the front-facing windows were worn, and more than a few of them were off their hinges. The kitchen had never been updated and still had a yellow linoleum floor and white tile counters. Over time, Drew and Katie painted, sanded, and replaced beaten and broken parts of the house until it took on a fairy-tale appearance. The deep red Dutch door entry stood out against the sky-blue paint and white trim on the house. Dark blue shutters framed the windows. The house even had a white picket fence. Drew used every penny of his military pay and all of his savings to muster the down payment. That and the very humiliating loan that Katie had to get from her father, who openly disdained Drew, put them in way over their heads. The house was small—three bedrooms and two baths, only twelve hundred square feet. A cramped backyard had just enough room for two young boys to get into acres of mischief and leave the space in constant disarray. Still, it was their home. It was perfect. It was everything Drew had dreamed of growing up in Salinas. The small agricultural town in Northern California had instilled in him a great sense of family and pursuit of the American dream. Katie was definitely the bonus. Drew knew he married outside of his social level and to a beauty way outside of his league.

The truck came to a stop, and Drew turned off the ignition. He leaned back in the seat and took a deep breath. A mind-clearing breath. The type of calming breath that he had been trained to use and perfected as a Marine sniper. The breath that would calm his nerves, lower his heart rate and allow him to coldly squeeze the trigger. In the driveway, he tried to clear his mind, but the mental process of unifying his body with his weapon and firing a lethal shot was somehow far easier than trying to calm himself from the crushing pressures of daily civilian life. The mortgage, the repairs to the house, the recent discovery of little Drew's learning disabilities, the cost of everything, the lack of money. Drew knew he couldn't tell Katie what he was thinking about doing. She would never understand. She would tell him that he was an idiot for even thinking about it. She, of course, was right. Katie would tell him she could ask her father for a loan. He would tell her no. She would tell him her father would help; it would be fine. He would say her father hated him. They would argue. She would cry. Drew would feel like crap.

Drew reached down the top of his Chargers T-shirt and grasped the hog's tooth hanging from a cord around his neck. In Scout Sniper School, Drew suffered through fifty days of wallowing through mud, lack of sleep, and general hellfire to get that tooth. The "tooth" was actually a rifle round connected to a nylon cord. It was a reward, a reminder, that he had made the shift from PIG, professionally instructed gunman, to HOG, hunter of gunmen. Drew's training taught him to control his emotions. The cleansing, mind-clearing breath had become his most useful tool.

Drew closed his eyes and took in another deep breath. The darkness always comforted him. The blackness became a purplish hue beneath his eyelids. Drew moved his pupils in a slow circular motion. The exterior world ceased to exist. Sound vanished. He slowly let the breath out and opened his eyes.

It's all good, he told himself.

Drew tapped the photo of his two sons with two fingers and got out of the truck. His heavy footsteps crushed the loose gravel and made a sound that stopped him. Looking up at his house, he had a bad feeling this might be the last time he saw it.

NINE

Something was wrong. Gerardo could not keep his eyes off the group of *polleros* gathered around the children. He was sitting with the group of twenty or so men and women as they waited for instructions.

"*Qué onda con los niños?*" Gerardo asked the old man next to him.

The man pulled the brim of his frayed ball cap down to shield his eyes as he looked away. All Gerardo could see was a white tangle of eyebrow under the side of visor. He caught the glance of a woman off to his side. She was in her thirties, a hooded pink sweat shirt that read Hollister zipped up to her neck. She had her mouth open as if she were about to say something. Her eyes looked troubled, and after a second or two, she looked away without speaking.

Gerardo put his hand on her shoulder.

"What are they doing with the children?" he asked.

She pulled away from his grasp. Gerardo could now see the worn features of a much older woman. He could tell she had made this journey many times before.

"*No sé . . .*" she said. "I don't know."

Gerardo could tell in the way she averted her eyes and looked around to see who was watching her that she knew something.

"*Tú sabes algo,*" Gerardo said, more a statement than a question. He reached out again to touch her shoulder and forced her to make eye contact.

"You know something," he said again.

The woman looked around again and lowered her voice.

"Son por los gueros, por los patrones."

Gerardo began to turn to look for the children when he felt a hard, crushing blow to his skull. The pain radiated from the back of his head to his mid-back. Lying face down in the coarse desert dirt, Gerardo could feel the warmth of blood running along the side of his face. He turned over, spat dirt out of his mouth and refocused his vision into the cloudless, star-filled night sky.

For an instant, despite the pain, he was thinking the sky was more beautiful than he could remember. The thought was interrupted by a kick to his ribs by one of the foot guides. The man was holding a matte black gun and pointing it at Gerardo.

"It's none of your fucking business, *puto*!"

The man drove his foot hard onto Gerardo's chest. On his back, Gerardo could not breathe. The remaining dirt in his mouth slid down his throat causing him to choke and cough.

"None of your business!" the man yelled again, then, turning to the rest of the group, "and none of the rest of your business."

Gerardo rolled to his side still coughing up dirt and blood. From the ground level, through the legs of the man with the gun, he could see the children, still tethered two by two, being led by men with guns.

None of my business, Gerardo thought to himself, none of my fucking business. But he could not keep the thought of his own eight-year-old daughter out of his mind.

TEN

Chino had set up the meeting at The Docks, a tacky, nautical theme bar in Chula Vista. It was a classic South Bay dive with fishing nets and lifesavers draped haphazardly on the walls. The lighting was dim and dingy, a stark contrast to the bright blue San Diego day outside. When Drew walked in it took a few moments to adjust his eyes, almost like walking into a movie theater. Chino and Chance were in a booth in the back looking like they were guilty of something. Chino spotted Drew and waved him over.

"*Qué onda*, Drew?" Chino extended a closed fist for a bump.

Drew gave him the obligatory bump and lowered himself into the booth.

"Wazzup, homey?" Chance said as he flipped his ball cap backward and held out his own meaty fist for a bump.

Drew did not respond and left Chance's fat fist hanging out for a few awkward seconds.

"No worries," Chance dropped his hand back on the table. "It's all good."

All Drew could think about as he sat across from Chance was that this doughy piece of shit thought he was some playa gangster in a rap video. Like I would be sitting anywhere with this cartoon character if I had any other prospects, he thought. Now, meeting him for the second time, Drew was convinced that the guy owned no other clothing but oversized NBA jerseys and crotch-drop sagging jeans. This time he was in a black Lakers jersey, not even the team's colors. Shit, Drew thought, this guy actually picked these clothes to wear.

A middle-aged waitress dressed in younger-than-middle-aged clothes, two sizes too small, wiggled her way over to the booth.

"What can I get for you, soldier boy?" she asked Drew. Even in civilian clothes and nonmilitary haircut, Drew couldn't shake the image.

"Shot of Patron and a Pacifico."

Drew knew he had to settle his nerves because everything about Chance rubbed him the wrong way. All his military training—his patience, deliberate and calculated movements, his instinct— screamed this was a bad idea. Spiderman had his spider sense, Drew had his sniper's sense. He could never lose it, but his situation over powered the obvious.

"Well, let's make a few things clear," Drew said as he noticed the waitress on her way with the drinks. He stopped talking and watched her put the beer and tequila shot on the table next to the Tecates that Chino and Chance had ordered earlier. She also set down a plate with two quartered limes.

"The salt is on the table," she said with a nod toward the napkin holder. "Let me know if you need any help with that."

Even in the dark, Drew could make out her stained smoker's teeth. Her crooked smile lingered for a second in Drew's vision even after she turned away. Drew grabbed the shot glass and tossed the tequila down. The familiar Patron burn rising in his throat gave Drew a certain calm. He bit down hard into the lime wedge. The sour and sweet juices sent the burn of the tequila back down his throat. Back to what he knew best. Clear his thoughts. Deep breath.

Eyes closed. Exhale. Eyes open. Same dreary bar. Same absurd blob sitting across the table.

"Like I was saying," Drew continued, "I don't know you, Chance. The only reason I'm here is because I need the money, and Chino says he can vouch for you."

Chino looked a bit uneasy after Drew mentioned vouching.

"Look, homey, I don't know shit about you and . . ." Chance stopped midsentence as he saw Drew laser beam his gaze at him.

Drew took a long gulp of Pacifico and put the bottle down off to the side. Nothing blocked Drew's line of sight, and Chance squirmed back in his seat.

"Two fucking combat tours, one Bronze Star, sniper school, twelve confirmed kills," Drew said deliberately. He leaned across the table.

"Only people who play fucking basketball should wear jerseys and then, only when they are playing, and make no mistake about this—I am not your homey. That's all you need to know about me, motherfucker."

Chance tugged at the jersey to examine the front as if he had not known that it said Lakers across the front.

"*Traanquilo*, Drew," Chino said, knowing Drew would never be comfortable with Chance.

Like it or not, Drew was committed to the deal. Although every fiber in his body screamed at him to walk away, the only way out seemed to be a pinhole of light at the end of a pitch-black tunnel. Chance, he realized dismally, was his only guide through the dark passage.

Drew took another deep breath. Looking around to see if anyone had noticed his tirade, he concluded that in this no-account bar in

Chula Vista, no one gave a rat's ass why three losers were here in the middle of the afternoon.

"Let's hear what you have to say," Drew said, "and without the play gangster talk."

Looking everywhere as if to make sure nobody in the empty bar was listening, Chance changed his posture from an uncomfortable squirm to a lazy slouch.

"I know this guy. He's from TJ," Chance leaned forward. "Actually, he's from Sinaloa."

"What's his name, and how do you know him?" Drew asked.

"Don't know his real name. They call him Caritas."

"What the hell does that mean?"

Chance had a bewildered look on his face and looked to Chino for help.

"It's a nickname, Drew," Chino said. "It means something like 'pretty boy.'"

"Yeah, yeah," Chance continued. "Anyways, Caritas runs a pollo outfit."

Like most people in border states, Drew knew "pollos" were people being smuggled into the United States. The stories of the cruelty to the undocumented crossers by smugglers and bandits were commonplace. People were stuffed into car doors and engine compartments. They were smuggled through the rugged mountains and deserts in Mexico and San Diego County. They were loaded into boats and forced to jump into the surf off Imperial Beach and as far north as La Jolla. They were herded through hidden drug tunnels. The common factor in all the methods was that the men, women, and children being smuggled were treated like human garbage. They were expendable.

Chino looked at Drew and could sense he was not cool with the idea.

"This is different, Drew. Just here Chance out."

"That's right, Drew, this is different," Chance chimed in.

"Mind telling me how?"

"These are special illegals," Chance lowered his voice. "These pollos are paying top dollar to cross. I think up to twenty grand a head."

Chance leaned back and smiled.

"What makes these guys so high class?" Drew asked.

"Who the fuck knows? Who cares, we get paid," Chance said, excitement in his voice.

"Why do they pay so much?"

"Guaranteed delivery. They've got a system. Money-back guarantee."

"What's our job?" Drew already knew what it would be.

"We are UPS, the brown," Chance snickered at his inside joke. "We pick up the brown and make the delivery."

"What's our end?" Drew found himself being pulled into the venture.

"Even better than I originally told you," Chance paused and looked around the room, "One thousand a head, dude! Each of us drives a vehicle. Six to eight per load. Three to four times a week. You do the math." Chance, feeling smug at the prospect, leaned back again in his seat and clasped his hands behind his head.

As much as he did not want to give this sad sack any respect, Drew couldn't help but start adding things up. He was thinking about mortgage payments, utility bills, credit cards, and dental work for his boys.

"How do we know that we are not smuggling in haji terrorists?" Drew asked in a serious tone.

Chance looked around the room as if one of the bar's aimless patrons had developed a sudden interest in their conversation.

"Who the fuck cares?"

"I care!" Drew said in a loud voice, and two old men drinking at the bar did sense a difference in their mundane lives and turned to look at him.

Chino reached over and placed his hand on Drew's arm.

"Stay cool, bro," Chino whispered.

Drew took a deep breath to calm himself, and it almost worked. The vibration of his phone inside the front pocket of his jeans startled him. He pulled the phone out and checked the flashing screen. HOME. HOME. HOME. It kept flashing. It was as if Katie knew he was up to something. Drew powered down the phone and returned it to his pocket.

"We could be transporting the next Osama bin Laden, and we wouldn't even know it. We could be responsible for the next 9/11." Drew willed his voice to be calm and measured and it was.

"The thing is," Chino said quietly as he angled himself across the table, "we won't know, we can't know."

"What are you saying?" Drew asked as he straightened in his seat.

"What I'm saying is that this operation is happening with us or without us."

"Someone's getting paid, homey," Chance added as if to end the argument.

"He's right, Drew. Dudes are coming across with or without our help. With our help means we get the money," Chino said with a sigh as he put both hands flat on the table.

"Someone's gonna do this, so it might as well be us," Chance said, a criminal tone to his voice that was different from his faux gangster posturing.

The last time Drew heard anyone say that was in Afghanistan before a mission that was poorly planned and exceedingly dangerous. That was the last thing the Humvee driver said before he took a bullet through the eye.

ELEVEN

Gerardo did his best to keep his eyes trained on the ground in front of him. He considered the gravity of his situation. Thirsty, tired . . . sitting cross-legged in the desert dirt and shrub with twenty people awaiting instructions. Instructions to stand, to walk, for permission to talk. His head still ached from the gun-butt blow, and dried blood was caked in his hair. Gerardo could not help but appreciate the irony of his injury. In a previous life, he had been a federal police detective in Culiacan. More times than he cared to remember, Gerardo had delivered the same blow to an uncooperative witness or suspect.

Ten years as a cop in Sinaloa's capital had placed him in regular contact with violent *narcos*, drug addicts, kidnappers, and other criminals. Not a day went by in Culiacan that he did not see or hear of a shooting or execution. As a result, he could distinguish between small-time street thugs and cartel *sicarios*. It became clear this was no ordinary border crossing. These *polleros* were not the type of traffickers commonly seen at the border. For starters, these men were heavily armed. Ten men for twenty or so poor laborers, some of them women, and twelve children? Four men had automatic rifles like the ones he used in the Mexican army and later as a federal police officer. All of them had handguns, the same model of nine-millimeter Glocks issued to the military. This was overkill. He kept coming back to thoughts of the children tethered two by two like animals being led to slaughter.

"*A pie, pendejos!*" shouted the bearded fat one in the front. "Get up."

All the *pollos* stood up, as did the children.

"*Vámanos!*" the leader said loudly as he pointed to what appeared to be a road off in the distance. Headlights flickered intermittently. Gerardo estimated it to be a good forty-minute walk. As they trudged down the trail, Gerardo saw one of the armed men do something that seemed out of place. The tall skinny one with the Raiders ball cap went to each of the children and began cleaning off their dirt-smudged faces with a damp rag.

TWELVE

"This was not a good idea," Drew kept thinking before Chance and Chino picked him up to drive out to meet the "money," as Chance called him. As they drove farther away from San Diego down a backcountry road near Tecate, the California border town just across from the much bigger Mexican city of the same name, Drew knew it was a bad idea. The inside of Chance's Silverado pickup seemed cramped with Drew in the front passenger seat and Chino folded into the rear jump seat. The inside of the vehicle reeked of the cheap Christmas tree deodorizers hanging from under the glove box that failed to hide the dank stench of cigarette butts in the ashtray.

The two-lane road snaked through the dry, low scrub of the mountains. The terrain reminded Drew of a mission in Yemen a few years back. The outside temperature hovered around ninety as the road seemed to radiate steam. Like a desert mirage, Drew thought. Inside the Silverado, the AC was cranked to near refrigerator level. Chance was one of those overweight guys who pumped the AC to full at all times no matter what the outside temperature.

"Why couldn't these guys meet us somewhere closer to San Diego?" Drew said, even though he knew the answer.

"Their money, their rules," Chance said, offering the only intelligent thing he had said all day.

They turned off the main road onto what looked like a fire trail. Chance was driving slowly, making an ash-white dust cloud behind the truck.

"Look," Chance said, "all I know is that this run is special. The man wants the best to ensure the transport."

"How can we be the best when we have never done it before?" Drew asked as he caught a glimpse of Chino in the mirror of the visor, he had folded down to reduce the blinding glare.

"Truth is," Chino said as he canted himself forward, "I have met these guys before."

"Shit, Chino! Why didn't you tell me?" Drew was upset. He looked over at Chance who was doing his best not get involved in a situation he clearly knew about.

"You see, Drew," Chino said, now with his Padres hat off, as if to be more serious, "I needed to check it out first before I brought you into this."

Chance was driving even slower, gripping the steering wheel hard and staring straight ahead.

"I need this, Drew. Shit, I haven't had work in nine months, and Sophia is starting to lose it."

"I am sure you didn't clear this with her," Drew said, the bitter taste of his own situation on his tongue.

"Of course not, neither did you. The point is that I can't do this without you," Chino put his hand on Drew's shoulder.

The truck came to a stop in front of an iron gate with a no-trespassing sign and secured with a heavy chain and padlock. Another sign on the gate, rusted yellow with black lettering, read "No Hunting." Several bullet holes were visible. Chance killed the engine, and Drew got out of the truck. The heat of the midday sun sizzled the skin on his arms. He was sweating instantly, and the Chargers T-shirt began to cling to his body. Drew didn't look back at the truck. He took a few steps toward the gate and looked out down the winding dirt road.

Still time to bail.

The truck doors opened behind him, and he could hear Chino and Chance get out.

"I know I'm asking a lot from you, and I will totally understand if you don't want anything to do with this," Chino said while studying the dirt and kicking up a tiny cloud with his boot.

The years in the Corps as partners meant a lot to both of them. Drew always had Chino as a shadow, he was always there. He knew the fear that Chino was dealing with under these conditions. The unknown, the danger. Drew could feel it.

"I have to do this," Chino said and patted Drew's shoulder again. "Just hear the man out."

Drew turned to speak. Over Chino's shoulder, he saw two SUVs coming down the road toward them leaving another trail of billowing dust.

THIRTEEN

Dirt had a way of equalizing every man, Gerardo thought. Here he was in the desert plodding through the clay-colored dirt to get to a place where he could labor in the dirt. For what? He thought of the last time he had such a keen awareness of dirt.

The outskirts of Culiacan. Off the highway to Los Mochis.

Standing behind El Cicatriz and his men, he could see Armando Guerrero kneeling in the dirt. Under the brutal August sun, temperature searing to 110 plus, the heat radiated from the bright red clay dirt. Armando's Chivas jersey was caked in the red dirt and blood. Armando kept his eyes down, knowing full well what was going to happen to him.

Gerardo had grown up with Armando. He had been to his birthday parties as a child. He knew his family. He knew his children. Gerardo also knew this was a necessary part of life in this hellhole he called home. Once you decided to become part of "*la vida*," then you had to accept inevitable consequences.

Gerardo made the decision when he took the first payment for his services to El Cicatriz. It wasn't a conscious decision. One night playing dominoes in El Botin, a local watering hole, Gerardo struck up a conversation with an acquaintance from secondary school. Gerardo was complaining of the low pay the detectives received. They put their lives on the line on a daily basis. All for 400 pesos a month.

"*Que madre*," Juan Manuel said.

Gerardo knew Juan Manuel was in the *narco* vida. Here in the bar, however, as long as you minded your own business, everyone got along.

"Los federales. Special Narcotics Enforcement Unit. That's the way to go." Gerardo squeezed a lemon slice over the opening of his Tecate can and then flicked a couple of dashes from the salt shaker. Gerardo took a long, deep draw off the can and closed his eyes as he swallowed.

"They wear masks, so no one knows who they are, everyone knows who we are. *Puta madre*, everyone knows where we live," Gerardo said and took another long drink.

Juan Manuel slid the bottle of añejo across the table to Gerardo.

"Now these *especialistas putos* are in town to steal the glory and make the news," Gerardo took a sip from the bottle and chased it with the beer.

"Where they going to be, 'mano?" Juan Manuel asked.

"*Tú sabes, buey*, I can't tell you that. Let's just say that Sunday might be a better day for all of you to go to church or call in sick."

Gerardo instantly regretted making the comment. He knew he should have kept his mouth shut. Too late, he thought. Fuck it. He hadn't named sources or given any locations. Gerardo took another drink from the añejo and went back to the game of dominoes.

A week later, when Gerardo was back in the bar, Juan Manuel came up to the table where he sat and slid an envelope across the table.

"El Jefe would like to thank you for your assistance last week."

Gerardo was frozen. He looked down at the envelope and then around the bar. No one seemed to be paying attention. The man he had been playing dominoes with left when Juan Manuel walked over.

"He would like to thank you for encouraging his employees to be good *catolicos* and attend church more often," Juan Manuel pushed the envelope closer to Gerardo.

Gerardo cupped the envelope with his forearm and slid it down onto his lap.

"Tell your jefe that a man who has God has everything he needs."

"I'm sure that when he calls, you will have the opportunity to do that for yourself," Juan Manuel said before dropping a cellphone on the table in front of Gerardo and walking out.

When Gerardo got back to his car, he opened the envelope. Inside were twenty U.S. one-hundred-dollar bills. And that was it. The money kept coming. At first just information about investigations and arrests. Later he was asked to pick up and deliver packages. This time, he was asked to pick up and deliver Armando Guererro to a deserted, trash-strewn field outside Culiacan, off that highway to Los Mochis.

Armando knew why he was being picked up. He pleaded with Gerardo to drop him off on the side of the road and give him just a twenty-minute head start. Give him the chance. For his kids. For the sake of their friendship. But Armando also knew Gerardo could not do that. Gerardo did his best to ignore him.

Now, watching Armando kneeling in the dirt, consigned to his fate, Gerardo knew he had crossed a line that he had long avoided. He had been a hardworking police officer. He helped people, provided a small sense of security in an otherwise chaotic and dangerous world. Now he was part of the chaos. Now he was the danger.

The dirt. That was what he remembered most. The way the dirt caked immediately to Armando's shirt and bloody face when he was forced to the ground. Mostly, however, he remembered the way the dirt shot up in a bright red cloud after El Cicatriz blew half of Armando's head into the ground.

That night, Gerardo stayed awake into the early morning hours. The shooting. Armando's pleas. The first envelope. *Plata o plomo.* No way out. But the last thing he thought about before he drifted off to sleep was dirt.

FOURTEEN

The black Escalade came to a stop at an angle behind the truck, blocking any exit. The cloud of dust was settling when all four doors opened at once. The driver—mid-thirties, dark skin, goatee, sunglasses—got out first and stood parallel to the vehicle facing Drew's group. The front passenger—heavy set, cleanshaven, a large, shiny Western-style belt buckle that seemed to be slicing into his overhanging belly fat—turned back to man the door behind him. The rear driver-side passenger got out and never turned in Drew's direction. He just walked directly away from the rear of the Escalade and stood in the middle of the dust looking down the road. The driver waited for the other rear passenger to step out. That man was clearly the boss as he was the slowest to exit and the most deliberate in his movements. Drew had been trained to assess targets from a distance, and he could tell by the body movements of the others and the confidence displayed by this man that he was in charge.

Drew looked over at Chino. Chino was doing his best to appear calm and unafraid but, like Drew, he was unaccustomed to facing down a potential danger without being armed or having some tactical advantage. Chance stepped in front of both of them and took a slouchy pose as the group approached.

Christ, this fat tub of lard is our mouthpiece?

"*Órale*," Chance said as he raised his right hand to a position that made him look like some wooden cigar store Indian. "*Qué onda, Caritas!*"

Silence. That was all Drew remembered about that first encounter. Silence. The Boss just stared at them. Not a word. While the others were dressed in *frontera* cowboy wear, the Boss was dressed like he was going to a nightclub. Drew could only assume this was Caritas. Here in this blistering heat and dusty road, he was wearing tight black slacks and a form-fitting black dress shirt. Drew didn't know a thing about men's dress shoes, but he could tell that these slip-on things with a silver buckle across the top were expensive. Drew could not see much of his face because he was wearing dark, oversized sunglasses with thick black frames. He could tell he was cleanshaven except for Elvis-like sideburns that traveled down past his ears. The man's hair was jet black and slicked back with some sort of grease that no doubt could repel water.

Silence for what seemed like minutes was finally broken when Caritas pulled the sunglasses low on his nose and looked directly at Drew.

"You the Marine," he said. More of a statement than a question.

Silence.

Drew took a step toward him. The cowboys behind Caritas moved toward Drew.

"You the pretty-boy boss?" Drew said as he analyzed the threat factor. One man wearing a bright white cowboy hat with a black band across the brim was reaching his right hand behind his back. Drew took a step forward, alongside Chance. He needed to make it clear that Chance did not speak for him.

Silence again . . .

. . . Until Caritas laughed and took off the sunglasses and propped them on top of his head. All Drew could think of was how greasy and smudged the lenses would be.

"That's what they call me."

"You speak English well," Drew said as he took a step back.

"La Jolla High class of 2000. Go *pinche* Vikings." Caritas offered a crooked smile as he scanned the group.

Drew's mind started to race. Shit, he thought, La Jolla High. Did he go to school with Katie? He couldn't remember exactly when his wife graduated from high school. That would be bad if they knew each other.

"Actually two Marines," Chance popped in, "both certified fucking war heroes. God damned killers of raghead and terrorist motherfuckers."

Drew squelched the overwhelming desire to cuff this loser up the side of the head.

The threat assessment going on his head was something Drew could not control. Three threats, three targets behind Caritas. Off to his right, Drew could see the handle of a firearm tucked directly to the right of the man's belt buckle. Drew also noticed the man's gut was hanging over the belt line and pistol grip. He would have to bend back and take a breath to pull the gun cleanly. That would cost the man a full second or two.

The second stood behind Caritas, gun stuffed behind his back on the beltline. Classic movie gangster style, which looked good but was entirely ineffective in a fight. Not only would he have to reach behind his back to pull the weapon, but he would also have to move a full four feet to his right to fire without hitting Caritas.

The third man was the problem. He was tall and lean. No large belt buckle, no wanna-be cocaine cowboy look. Even though his eyes were hidden behind bright mirrored sunglasses, Drew could tell he was the one with training. Although he could not see his eyes behind the glasses, Drew could sense the man was looking directly at him, no doubt doing his own risk assessment. The footwear gave him away. Military tactical boots. While the others were dressed for an afternoon in a bar, this man was ready for action. His weapon, a Glock nine-millimeter, was on his right hip. The strap on the holster was unhinged. It was as if he were daring someone to force him to draw his weapon. He stood five feet to the left of Drew, clear line of fire, free of any obstructions.

"So, I've been told that you two are the shit . . ." Caritas flipped the glasses back down off his head, "a team."

Chino looked over at Drew and waited for him to say something.

"We can get things done," Drew said. He was getting antsy because the clear threat had moved parallel to him on his right.

"That's good, *muy bueno*," Caritas said with a nod.

Before Drew could react, the man on his right had the gun out and pointed at his head from about three feet away.

"*Quieto, pendejo!*" he said. With one quick step, the gun was against Drew's head.

Drew slipped into combat mode. Options. The man was close enough for a crushing blow to his sternum. Drew could deliver an elbow that would drop the arm and the gun. Drew figured this badass had never dealt with anyone with legitimate hand-to-hand combat skills, so his guard was down. The other two, however, were now a problem. Fatty had pulled his gun out from somewhere under his gut, and the second had moved out from behind Caritas. Drew thought this through very quickly. He had never met Caritas and never botched one of his jobs. Caritas had no reason to kill him. This was a show of force. Drew relaxed the muscles in his forearm and waited for the next move.

Caritas motioned to the fat man. "*Carteras, Gordo!*"

The fat one somehow maneuvered his gun back into his waistband and came behind them to pat the pockets of their pants. He pulled out Chino's and Drew's wallets and handed them to Caritas.

Caritas turned his back and walked toward the front of the Escalade. He emptied the contents of both wallets on the hood. He was silent for a minute or so as he arranged some of the items alongside each other. From a distance Drew could see his driver's license next to a photo of his wife and kids. Caritas reached into his rear pocket, pulled out his cellphone, and took pictures of the items on the hood. He then took all three of their driver's licenses and slid them into his wallet.

"No disrespect, *amigos, pero,* you have seen me. There is no turning back on this now. Not a question of being in or not. You are all," Caritas was looking directly at Drew, "most definitely in."

"We know where you live," Fatty couldn't help himself. "We know what your kids look like."

The muscles and tendons in Drew's forearms twitched, firing with violence that begged to be unleashed.

"*No se preocupen,* don't worry, boys," Caritas said as he swept the wallets and other items off the hood of the Escalade and onto the dirt. The dust cloud was still swirling as Caritas walked toward Drew and Chino.

"Do the job. Don't fuck around. Get paid. *Muy simple, que no?*"

Drew looked over at Chino and Chance. Both looked frozen. Neither moved nor said a word.

"This is a one-time deal. No dope. Nobody hurting anybody," Drew said while he reached down to pick up his wallet. The picture of Katie and the boys was half buried. Katie's face was covered by the red clay dirt. He knew what her eyes would be telling him if he could see them.

"No drugs, mi amigo. This is a much more precious cargo. No one gets hurt unless they need to be. Do this right, and no one needs to get hurt. *Comprendes?*"

"We cool, *ese*," Chance said and let out a nervous laugh.

"Tomorrow, nine p.m. at the Indian casino off the Eight. Be in the parking lot, don't be late."

Caritas turned and walked back to the Escalade. His three men backed away toward the SUV, the one with the mirrored glasses kept his gaze on Drew the entire time. No smile, no frown, just a blank slate behind silver mirrors. He continued even as the vehicle started to move away. It seemed like the dust cloud the car had made coming in had barely cleared as the new storm of red dust rose and swirled as they drove off.

The three of them stood speechless for a few moments.

"This shit just got real," Chino said as he watched the car drive off.

Drew said nothing. He dusted off the picture of his wife and kids and slid it into his wallet. He walked to the truck contemplating the dangers that he just created for himself and his family.

FIFTEEN

The blood-red sun had begun to rise over the craggy hills to the east. The low shrubs separating the large boulders gave way to large swaths of white sand. The last cool sliver of evening was hanging on, but Gerardo could feel the beginning of what would be a searing day on the desert floor.

The landscape was harsh yet strikingly beautiful. The desert looked dry, desolate and, to him, like a place where you went to die. The crimson-streaked landscape of shrubs and boulder appeared to awaken with the movement of birds and shadows.

The *polleros* were very active. They moved through the group and roused the men and women to their feet.

"*Levántense, pendejos!*"

Gerardo rose. He watched the others stir and gather their belongings. Most carried long-handled mesh bags stuffed with sweaters and food. Gerardo had nothing to carry but a liter-size bottle of water and a plastic bag with a loaf of bread and a bean and cheese burrito. He took his New York Yankees hat off and ran his fingers through his matted hair and around the sweatband inside the hat to check the items he had hidden. Twenty-five carefully folded one-hundred-dollar bills. This was everything he had after leaving town before receiving a second visit from one of Cicatriz's enforcers.

He tried not to attract attention to what he was doing. The evening had made Gerardo wary of his surroundings, and he became somewhat disoriented. He looked behind him toward the rising sun. At the instant he turned, he noticed the dust in the distance rising. As the sun rose higher above the hills in the east, the rays beamed over the area where the dust was swirling and lit it up.

That's when he saw it.

It was just an instant, but it was clear. From a distance of about fifty yards, Gerardo could see one of the armed *polleros* with his back to him. He held up the end of a long, wooden plank, and two of the children who had been traveling in pairs over the course of the evening stood nearby and looked at him. They were still tied together at the hands. Left hand to right hand. The man motioned to them with his free arm, and they walked forward and down into the dirt. Then, as quickly as they started to move the man let the plank fall. A blast of dust rose in the air, and the children were gone.

Gerardo took an instant to recognize that he had seen something he wasn't supposed to see. He spun quickly back to his group, turning his eyes downward. As he turned, Gerardo caught a glimpse of one of the armed men looking at him.

Did he see me?

Gerardo took a knee and started to fiddle with his shoelaces. He dared not to look up. There was no mistaking what he saw. Children being hidden underground.

He knew that when he looked up, the *pollero* would be staring directly at him to determine whether he had seen anything. Gerardo knew what he saw was something out of the ordinary, even in this illegal world. These children were not simple *pollos*. They were not the children of mothers and fathers anxiously awaiting their arrival. These children were going to be used for something. They were going to be sold.

Gerardo unlaced his boot and pulled his right foot half out. Pretending to search inside for a pebble bought him a few seconds to compose himself. But the longer he delayed, the more suspicious he looked.

A shout from one of the other *polleros* brought everyone to attention.

"*A la tierra, todos!*" he yelled in the loudest hushed voice possible.

Everyone dropped to the ground. Gerardo hit the dirt but lifted his head enough to look down the road. He saw the yellow running lights of a vehicle coming in their direction from about a half a mile away. The only vehicles way out here at this time were *la migra* or vigilante gringos. Either one was not good for the group. Given what he had seen of the children and the way the *polleros* were armed, this became a dangerous situation.

Dead silence on the trail. The entire group was partially hidden from the view of the oncoming vehicle by a low hill. The sun had risen enough to begin to bake the ground, and Gerardo could feel the rays scorching the back of his neck. The seconds dragged until the vehicle made an abrupt right turn about a quarter of a mile away and accelerated.

No one was about to move until they were ordered to do so. With all the crossers lying face down in the dirt, all six *polleros* rose and gathered to the side of the trail. Gerardo followed them with his eyes and shifted his head to keep an eye on the one who had seen him watching the children. They seemed to be arguing while the leader was speaking on a cellphone a few feet away.

Gerardo resisted, with every nerve in his body, the overwhelming urge to look back and see what was happening where he had last seen the children. Gerardo kept his eyes forward on the group of armed men. With the sun a few degrees higher in the east, Gerardo could see that the *pollero* who had seen him was just a boy. He looked no older than eighteen. Wearing an El Tri *fútbol* jersey and Chargers ball cap pulled down low, he could not make out any of his facial features except sparse facial hair on the side of his cheek. The slim body and smooth skin betrayed his youth.

The boy was talking to the others when the man on the phone put it in his back pocket and pointed to the boy. In an instant, the boy began a measured run back down the road toward where Gerardo had last seen the children.

Gerardo closed his eyes and breathed out in relief knowing this young man was now distracted and would forget what he had seen. All Gerardo had to do was disappear into the faceless group of crossers. They were unremarkable gardeners, laborers, cooks, and housekeepers. Looking around him, they were all still frozen, lying face down as instructed by the guides. To Gerardo they looked like victims of a roadside ambush, lying dead in the sun-bleached dirt.

Dirt. Pinche dirt.

SIXTEEN

He had done the math in his head. Drew was going to make three runs and, at the rate per head Caritas offered, he would collect almost eight thousand dollars. That would cover the last two months' mortgage with some extra for the current month. He would never get this past Katie without a believable story. He knew she would call Chino's fiancée to confirm the job. No one he knew made eight thousand dollars in three days.

In the end, it was Chino who came up with the most believable cover. They had been contracted by a private security company in Mexico to consult on military reconnaissance and surveillance. The job paid cash and, because it was in Mexico, it was off the radar.

"Sounds pretty *narco* sketchy to me," Katie said, although she seemed to resist only mildly.

They were standing at the kitchen island. Drew looking down at the sink hoping Katie was not trying to read his eyes.

"Everything is sketchy down there," Drew said. "That's why the security people need the training."

"Is it dangerous?" Katie asked, but she knew the answer.

"Couldn't be worse than the shit in Iraq, besides I'll have Chino with me. You know he's got my back."

Drew was getting the impression that this was going to work. Maybe Katie believed him. Maybe she wanted to believe him. Drew knew Katie was keenly aware of their financial situation and eight thousand dollars would get them out of the hole.

"I'll only be gone a week, and you know we could use the money."

Drew hated lying to Katie. Not so much because it was a lie. There was more to it than that. It was a lie that was, in fact, dangerous. It was a lie he might never be able to take back. It was a lie that might take him away from his children.

Katie came around the island to Drew and put her arms around his neck. She took a deep breath and leaned her face into his chest.

"Do what you need to do, Drew. Be safe."

Drew reached his hand around the back of her neck and gave it a light squeeze. He took in the familiar and comforting aroma of her soft hair.

"I promise, darlin'."

A noise from the boys' room sounded like they were fighting. Drew let go of Katie and started toward the room.

"I got this," Drew said as he walked away.

"Drew . . ." Katie said just above a whisper.

Drew stopped and turned back.

Katie's back was turned to Drew and she gazed out the kitchen window into the darkness.

"Don't do anything stupid."

It was clear to Drew that she didn't want a response from him. This was more of a plea than a demand. Drew turned and made his way to the boys' room.

Don't do anything stupid. Deep inside, he knew it was already too late for that.

Katie remembered back to the conversation she and Drew had in the kitchen four months earlier. Katie had been doing her best to manage the finances, juggling bills, minimum payments on credit cards, stretching every penny that she could. Drew was still only working part time, and they had not been able to make the last mortgage payment. She tried to remain positive.

Katie was making dinner and the boys were in the living room watching Cartoon Network when Drew came bounding through the door. His recently dour demeanor had been upgraded to an almost giddiness she had never seen. Drew was excited to tell Katie he had run into his old gunnery sergeant at the firing range. The gunny had told him about an investment that had some serious potential.

Katie was wary of anything involving an investment of their savings and even more apprehensive of recommendations from friends.

"Investments Drew, really? It's not like you hold some type of finance degree from Wharton."

Katie immediately regretted mentioning Wharton, and not because Drew would have no idea who or what Wharton was. Her father had graduated with an MBA from the Wharton School of Business at the University of Pennsylvania. She grew up with the diploma hanging framed in his home office and with her father touting the superiority of MBAs from Wharton every chance he could.

"Well," Drew said with both hands on the kitchen island that separated the two of them, "I don't know anything about Wharton, but Gunny says that his uncle has a spot for him on the ground level of a significant medical invention."

Good God, she thought. A sophisticated financial transaction and medical technology. Drew had no experience in either.

"What type of invention?"

"Some sort of medical vaccine device that costs pennies to make and can retract into its own disposable container." Drew seemed uncertain of the details, but that seemed to have little effect on his enthusiasm.

"Hasn't that been done already?"

Creases appeared in Katie's face. She knew the conversation was heading toward Drew suggesting they invest their savings in the venture. Katie had grown up with dinner table conversations about clients falling for investment scams built around the next great medical invention. Her father would laugh derisively at the thought of amateurs trying to get rich quick.

Still, Katie knew that some people were able to avoid the many schemes and hit it big with the right investment. Her thoughts raced as she considered consulting her father. The calculation didn't take long. He would once again show utter disdain for Drew's financial planning attempts. He would remind her that she married someone who had enlisted in the military, not a banker.

Katie knew Drew would not be distracted from the proposal's scent.

"From what I understand, it has been done before," Drew said feeling excited about his relaying the results of his research, "but no company has been able to manufacture the product with any sort of efficiency."

"What's different about this company?"

"It's small," Drew responded quickly. "Just the founder, his chief engineer, two or three research scientists and a working *maquiladora* in Tijuana."

"Why is that good?"

"Less interference from the board of directors and other large corporation crap." Drew was hoping that his simplified explanation made sense to Katie.

"How much, are you thinking of investing?"

"Gunny says that the minimum unit is twenty-five thousand."

Katie could hardly breathe.

"That's all of our savings," Katie said in almost a whisper. "You're not working full time now, and we are already behind on the mortgage."

"I know. I know," Drew said as walked over to the refrigerator. He paused for a second to look at the photo of Katie and the boys at Legoland before opening the door. He pulled out two Pacificos and walked back to the island. Katie was speechless. Drew held both bottles in one hand and reached into a cabinet drawer for an opener. When Drew popped off the caps, they made a metallic ring against the sink. He turned back to Katie and placed one beer in front of her. He took a deep drink from the other.

"The thing is, the device is geared for completion and production in three months. Gunny's uncle says that it will be announced at a major medical conference right here at The Scripps Research Institute and then it is going to explode."

"Have you even met any of these people?"

"Well…," Drew pulled back a bit from the island, "I know that Gunny is a pretty conservative dude, and he told me that he cashed out his retirement to invest. He told me that his uncle told him to go all in."

"All in?" Katie did not like the sound of that phrase.

"All in!" Drew said. "Do you think his uncle would screw over his own blood?"

Katie could just picture her father in his home office. Oversized mahogany desk. High-back leather tufted chair. Photos of stuffy old relatives, all men, whom she had never met. Something about that office, even now as an adult, made her feel so insignificant. When she and her father were in the room, she knew they were standing on the same floor, yet it seemed to her that he was always talking down to her. She knew he would tell her she needed to do her "due diligence" on the investment. He would tell her that she needed to contact outside sources to track the reliability of the information on which she was basing her decision to invest. Never, he would tell her, invest in something because someone else is investing everything they had.

How could she deny Drew? He seemed so excited. Drew always had big dreams of finding the magic bullet to a comfortable life. After he left the Corps, Drew did his best to find work. Nothing was beneath him. He would dig ditches at construction sites, temporary work at the Home Depot, whatever work he could find. He was looking for the one job that would provide stability for his family and make him feel good about going to work. As much as a down-to-earth, hard-working American male that he was, his dream of a spectacular financial victory endured. She knew she could not talk him out of this. If she suggested that she speak to her father about it, Drew would be crushed. It would snuff out the light she saw gleaming in his eyes as he spoke about what they could do with the money.

"Well, baby," Katie began to smile, "you know I love you."

Drew was about to speak, but Katie gestured with her open hand to keep him from talking.

"The way I see it, we are in this together, and if you feel like this is the right thing for us, then I am with you all the way."

Drew didn't say anything. He put his beer down and came around to Katie. He held her tight and whispered.

"Thanks, Katie. I love you."

Three months later, their world collapsed. Katie came into the kitchen early on a Saturday morning. The boys were still in bed. Drew was sitting at the kitchen table staring out the window. His phone was the only thing on the table.

"Hey, baby," Katie moved slowly to Drew. "Is everything okay?"

He lowered his head into his open hands.

"Drew, what's wrong?"

Drew slid his phone across the table.

"You need to read this."

Katie took a few slow steps to a chair and sat down. Drew was not looking at her. She took the phone and looked warily at the screen. Drew had the browser open to the Chronicle News Service. The headline smashed into her.

Medical Inventor Indicted on Fraud Charges.

Katie put the phone down, not wanting to read more.

"Our guy?" Katie knew the answer.

Drew still could not answer her.

Katie picked up the phone again and read the article. The allegations included wire fraud, mail fraud, and money laundering. According to the United States Attorney prosecuting the case, the investment was essentially a Ponzi scheme. The owner of the company solicited investments from individuals, offering them false and misleading data and research to make it appear as if the device was ready for production. Investors who questioned the viability of the project were paid returns through other investors' money. No device was ever produced. There were no plans or patents for the device. According to the article, the company's accounts were frozen and it was unknown if law enforcement was able to locate over fifteen million dollars of private investor money.

Katie dropped the phone on the table. She felt like throwing up. All their money was gone.

They hardly spoke with each other over the next week. Drew was scrambling to set up job interviews. He was able to get part-time work at a Santee trucking company but the pay was barely enough to cover food and utilities. The mortgage started to back up. They were now three months behind on the home loan, and property taxes were due. The tension in the house over finances was crushing them both. Katie decided she needed to do something. She knew that Drew would hate her for it, but she needed to talk to her dad about a loan.

As usual, her father treated their conversation like a business meeting. Rather than just speak to her at the family home, he had Katie meet him at the Varsity Club. The club was a holdover from the old boy's network of San Diego. Admission only by member recommendation and club vote. The club provided a restaurant and private meeting rooms for power broker backslapping and deal making. The club occupied the top two floors of a downtown high-rise with 360-degree views of the city and ocean. Katie had been there before and knew what to expect. She looked through her closet and picked out a bright but classy Kate Spade dress. She made sure she matched it with the purse her mother gave her for Christmas and the Tiffany diamond pendant her father bought for her when she graduated from high school.

Katie arrived at the Varsity Club ten minutes before she was expected, and her father was already there. He was seated at a table by the window. Katie gave a quick wave and smile. Her father, polite as always, stood up and waited for her to walk over. He was still handsome in his mid-sixties. He had a full head of white and gray hair cut in a style that you would expect in a corporate boardroom. He was wearing a deep blue blazer, crisp white button-down shirt and blue striped tie. He held his arms out for a hug as Katie approached.

The usual family pleasantries soon gave way to the serious subject matter. After Katie finished her summary, her father was silent. He looked down at a glass of Tullamore Dew neat, his usual. He took a short drink.

"I cannot believe after all you have seen and learned from being raised in my household, you would even entertain the idea that your husband," he paused, "Drew, would have the intellectual capability of analyzing a high-risk investment."

"But we had inside . . ." Katie started to say.

"There's no such thing," he raised his voice but maintained his demeanor. "Inside information is what con men tell their marks they have or, if it is real, is the type of information that can land you in prison."

"But Drew's gunny —"

"Good God, Katie," he interrupted, "need I remind you that you married a soldier, not quite the intellectual giant."

Katie began to tear up.

"Oh, don't start that. You are not a little girl."

Katie did not respond.

"I can't keep bailing you out every time your lug of a husband decides that he has a can't-miss way to make money," he said as he took another sip of the drink. "I told you when you married that soldier —"

Katie had been silent, but her anger reached the point of no return.

"Listen to me dad. I love you and mom, even though sometimes I find it difficult to do so. That will never change. You need to understand that I married Drew because I love him. I loved him from the first night that I met him. We have two beautiful children together, and we are raising them to be good people. Drew tries his hardest to provide for his family and this . . ." she couldn't come up with a name for it, "this was a big mistake."

Tears welled up in both her eyes, and she did her best to dab them with her white cloth napkin. She placed the napkin down and looked out the window. Her view of downtown swept over Coronado and down to Mexico. She paused and looked back at her father.

"I came here to ask for help from my father, desperately needed help. Help for *your* grandchildren. But instead I get a lecture on what a piece of garbage I married. Well, Dad," Katie lowered her voice but remained forceful, "my husband is not a soldier. He is a Marine. He enlisted to serve this country out a duty and loyalty to this country. He has put his life in harm's way on many occasions. You sleep secure in your bed each night because of men like Drew. Instead of belittling me for marrying him, you should be congratulating me. Drew has more character and dignity than you will ever know. You have spent your life in these rooms with other men moving money and enriching each other. Drew has been in the dirt and the muck so that you and your," she looked around the room, "friends can continue this charade you call life."

Katie's father looked around the elegant room, concern on his face. Outbursts like this were unseemly, even if no one could hear what his daughter was saying.

"I'll tell you what, Dad," Katie placed her napkin back on the table. "You're right I can't keep coming to you for help, and I will never do it again. I will not allow you to berate and insult my husband, the father of your grandchildren, ever again. Drew and I will figure a way out of this problem. We will do it without your help. We don't need you."

Katie got up and started toward the exit. She did not look back at her father. She never told Drew about the meeting.

SEVENTEEN

Drew picked up Chino and Chance at the same low-life bar where the three had met before. Something about this place—the people inside, the bartender with his crooked teeth and slicked back dirty hair, the gum-smacking older waitress—all screamed low-level criminality. Drew knew he had gone too far. He had met Caritas face to face. Drew knew what he looked like. More importantly, Caritas knew where he lived and how to find his family. Drew was pot committed to this plan, and he knew he did not have the best hand at the table.

There was little talk in the booth as all three tried to distract themselves from what lay ahead. Chance was carefully peeling the label off his dripping cold Budweiser like it was valuable artwork. Chino scrolled through phone messages looking for something interesting to read. When you are unemployed, he had told Drew, no one is sending you important messages. Drew was looking out the window behind him, spinning the shot glass of Patron absentmindedly with his right hand.

Nothing to do but think. Something weighed on Drew's mind that he could not shake. A few years earlier, Drew had been asked to go dinner with a friend from his unit who was in San Diego. His friend, Ronnie Castro, was meeting his father for dinner. Castro's father was a well-known criminal defense attorney in the city. Castro used to tell him he grew up reading about his father representing murderers, gang members and white-collar thieves in the newspapers and watching him sling the "my client welcomes his day in court" thing on the TV news. Drew had met him before, and the promise of a big fat Morton's steak, drinks, and stories on the old man's dime was a no-brainer.

Dinner began with the usual banter between father and son and slowly, after two martinis for the older Castro, devolved into a pulp fiction description of criminals, overreaching police tactics, and the danger of Mexican border towns.

"The thing about the border," Joaquin Castro said in a lowered voice as he cut into his thick, bloody steak, "is that it will never be secure."

"Here we go," Ronnie said. He looked over at Drew with a raised eye.

"The government drops a billion dollars on the war on drugs, which means the war on Mexicans, but it accomplishes nothing," Joaquin said, his fork impaled in the oversized ribeye as he reached for his martini.

Drew could never understand the allure of almost straight vodka, but somehow felt inferior as he sipped a pale-colored Pacifico. He had it in a glass, and he wondered if that provided him with a little more class.

"Truth is, boys, as long as drugs are illegal in this country, cartels will make sure they get into the United States. As long as money can be made, someone will step up and deliver the goods," Joaquin sucked down the last of the martini, then chewed and swallowed the olive for good measure.

"Are they really as bad as they show them in the movies?" Drew asked. The idea of real-life crime bosses was something foreign to him.

"Listen," Joaquin said with a raised finger to order another round for the table, "these guys come from nowhere. They know they are not going to live long lives. Most are resigned to it. They know that there is always going to be some younger street hood or *campesino* willing to put their own life on the line for the promise of a better, if not shorter life. What do they have to lose?"

Drew listened and felt stuffed from his own Flintstones-size steak.

"I had a client who had to work off a drug bust for the feds. He provided some very useful information for them. So much so that they were working on getting some of his family members into the U.S. with status papers. One day, while he was eating down in Chula Vista, four men walked in and dragged him out of the restaurant, in front of his fucking family."

Joaquin lowered his voice as the waiter arrived with the drinks.

"In front of an entire fucking restaurant in the United States of America! They didn't give a shit who saw them."

Joaquin's face seemed to become somber.

"The next day, they found him hanging from an overpass in TJ within sight of the border, facing the US side, with his dick, balls and all, shoved into his mouth."

Joaquin faced Drew.

"The TJ cops yellow-taped the area where he was hanging but left him there for four hours before they cut him down. Motherfuckers. Anyone driving into the United States from Mexico would have to pass under him."

Ronnie was chomping away at his steak like he heard the story a thousand times.

"The answer to your questions is . . ." Joaquin said as he swallowed half of the new martini. "It's not even close."

Drew had hardly thought about that dinner for years. Now, sitting in a run-down bar with his best friend and some idiot he met only a few days ago, it was all he could think about.

EIGHTEEN

"*Tu sabes lo que va a pasar*," the old man said and gave a knowing nod of his head toward the children who were emerging from the underground hold.

Gerardo tried to keep his speaking to a minimum in earshot of the *polleros*, so he gave the old man a shoulder shrug.

The man took off his battered LA Dodger cap, worked the bill with veiny hands and put it back on his head.

"*Lo van a vender*," he said with a defeated tone.

Sell the children, Gerardo thought, since when did they start selling kids?

In his years in Culiacan on both sides of the law, Gerardo had seen so many instances of human depravity that he could not imagine anything new. As much as he tried to shake it, Gerardo had law enforcement embedded in his DNA. In his mind he started the rudimentary deductive reasoning: The children were all about the same age, six to eight years old. They were bound together in pairs, boy-girl. They were kept clean by the *polleros*. All six of the girls had been changed out of the clothes that they had been slogging through the desert in and were in new dresses. Even the boys had been changed into new, clean clothes, and their hair was combed.

Gerardo tried not to consider the inescapable conclusion.

"*Oye, viejo*," Gerardo whispered to the old man. "*Adonde van?*"

The question was more of a mental suggestion for himself than the old man, who would not know the ultimate destination of the children.

"*Pues*," the old man said as he looked at the dirt, "*a los jefes*."

Los jefes. The bosses. The catch-all Mexican word for Americans with money. *Los jefes* gave them work. *Los jefes* allowed them to break their backs in the fields for minimum wage, clean toilets at large houses, cook food for their spoiled children. *Los jefes* drove expensive SUVs, and their wives shopped for whatever they wanted, whenever they felt like it.

Gerardo looked back at the five *polleros* left standing with the children. One was on a cellphone and pointed off in the distance down the dirt road on which they were standing. It was still only a few minutes after sunrise, but the sun was losing its orange-red hue and transitioning to bright white. The waves of heat were becoming more noticeable. In the distance, Gerardo could now see a cloud of dust making its way in their direction.

"*Aparanse todos*." The *pollero* wearing a white cowboy hat with a thick black band across it used both arms to signal to the group to stand.

Gerardo knew they were behind schedule. The transport to the vehicles should have been done at night. Daylight would make the movement of vehicles more visible to the Border Patrol. This next stage would be hurried.

Three vehicles pulled up in front of the *polleros* standing in the road. The first vehicle was a delivery truck with Chinese lettering and Ling Tsau Seafood Co. written on the side. The second vehicle was another delivery truck with a moving company name that Gerardo could not make out. The third vehicle was a brand-new

Ford F-350 pulling a sleek trailer. The side of the trailer read Anderson Racing. Stickers for motorcycle parts lined both sides of the trailer. The combination truck and trailer seemed out of place because they looked new.

The truck and trailer passed Gerardo on his right and continued down the dirt trail, and the two delivery trucks pulled up in front of the group of migrants. A man wearing a Chivas USA ball cap stepped up in front of the group. His facial features were blurred because the sun was directly behind him. The only thing visible was the mirrored lenses of the aviator-style sunglasses he was wearing.

"*Ojos aquí!*" he shouted, clearly intending that no one look back to where the truck and trailer had gone.

Gerardo knew the children were going to be loaded into the trailer and he knew, of course, they were not a usual load of migrants. As he looked at the group of poor travelers beside him, Gerardo could not help but marvel at how docile and subservient fear had made them. With his body tensed, daring itself not to turn around, he knew he was just like everyone else. Not my problem.

At that instant, Gerardo looked up and caught a clear image in the mirrored glasses of the man standing a few feet in front of him. With his senses heightened by fear, the images were as clear as if the man were wearing tiny television screens. Gerardo could see the trailer. The children were lined up behind it. He could see them being herded into a lower part of the trailer through an opening under the rear door. They crawled in on their stomachs one by one. Gerardo counted twelve of the children now concealed in a compartment under a very expensive looking racing trailer.

Gerardo's concentration was broken when another of the *polleros* shoved him forward from behind.

"*Todos adelante!*"

The group moved toward the two delivery trucks. Gerardo was ordered to step into the truck with the Chinese lettering. The truck was full of frozen fish and other boxes with Chinese brand names written across them. The interior was cold and bit hard against his skin. A path was cleared toward the back of the truck where an open space about five feet wide appeared behind a false wall.

"Back up to the wall!" the *polleros* yelled.

Gerardo felt crushed against the twenty or so crossers herded into the refrigerated trailer. The smell of stale cigarette and human sweat permeated the compartment into which he was crammed with the others. There was no room to sit. There was barely room to stand. As the false compartment door was shut, everything became pitch black. There was nothing left to do but stand and wait for the next stop.

As the truck bucked and pitched forward, the crossers packed into the compartment squeezed and stumbled against each other. In the dark, Gerardo could only think about where the children were being sent. More troubling for him was why they were being sent.

NINETEEN

All three men waited in the truck in the early dawn light. Drew's truck was backed into some shrub and obscured beneath a scraggly manzanita tree. From this position, the truck was hidden from aerial view and was off the dirt road. Drew knew the Border Patrol had helicopters as well as trucks on mountain ridges to view the valley floors.

The waiting was the hard part. It gave Drew time to think about what he was doing. It all felt wrong. There was no good end to this.

"I got a bad feeling about this, Chino," Drew said as he pushed his back nervously against his seat.

"It ain't no thing, Drew. Just a little drive and we're done."

"Something tells me that the pretty boy psychopath that has our identifications and home addresses is not going to let it be," Drew said. He scanned left to right across the valley floor looking for movement.

Chino turned to speak when he noticed a dust cloud down the dirt road from Drew's left.

Chino slapped Drew's shoulder and motioned to the vehicle moving their way.

The truck and trailer came into view with a Ford F150 following behind. As the vehicles came to a stop, Drew noticed the trailer appeared to be relatively new. The cover of being off-road racers or drivers was never discussed with them and seemed to be something that should have been researched in case law enforcement stopped them. *One more thing to go wrong.*

"Looks like we're desert rats," Chance said mostly to himself.

"Good thing we're dressed for it," Drew said. He looked around the cab of his pickup and realized that a former Marine wearing cowboy boots, a chino-Latino sidekick and a wanna-be gangster in oversized NBA wear did not look remotely like anyone who would use this high-end trailer.

The truck and trailer came to a stop, and Drew could see a black Jeep Cherokee also come to a stop some twenty-five yards behind the trailer. Two men got out of the truck. One was the fat ranchero cowboy they had seen earlier with Caritas. The other was the more dangerous one with the mirrored glasses. He motioned to his overweight companion with his hand for the keys. With keys in hand, he walked over to Drew's truck.

"Chance," Drew said while looking in the rearview mirror, "you stay in the truck."

Chance did not protest.

Chino got out of the truck and walked to the back and met up with Drew, who got out on his side.

"Guess now is not the right time to tell you that I am a little bit freaked out," Chino said. He took off his aviators and wiped them on his T-shirt.

"That, my friend, is a fact." Drew kept his eyes on the enforcer. "Too late for second thoughts."

Drew and Chino walked in the direction of the trailer and met up with the man with keys.

"This is very easy. *Muy fácil, amigos,*" the man said as he craned his head around Drew to look at Chance in the truck.

Drew could see his distorted reflection in the man's mirrored sunglasses as the guy dug into his shirt pocket to pull out a yellow sticky note.

"This truck goes to this address," he said and waved the note a few inches from Drew's face.

"When you get there, call the phone number on the note, and they will tell you how you will be getting home."

"What's in the trailer?" Drew asked.

"None of your *pinche* business!"

"How do we know that . . ."

"You don't, *puto*! Understand?"

Drew was about to say something when Chino put his hand on his Drew's shoulder.

"It's cool Drew, let's just get this over with."

"Listen to your amigo," the man said as he pasted the note on Drew's chest.

Drew took a step back and pulled the note off his chest. How easy would it be to bury an elbow in this low life's throat? But he kept moving backward.

"*Bien viaje, pendejos!*" the man said as he also backed away.

Drew turned to get back to the driver's side of the truck when the man yelled back at them from a distance.

"Remember, *putos*," he yelled, "don't look inside the trailer. Ever!"

The words ran through his head over and over as he backed his own truck further into the manzanita. He motioned for Chino to come over and help him field cover the truck with loose branches and brush. He had no idea when they would make it back to pick up the truck or, for that matter, whether they would make it back at all.

Don't look inside the trailer. Don't look inside the trailer. No matter how many times he said it, the desire to know what he was carrying made him feel sick.

TWENTY

The stink inside the delivery truck was crushing Gerardo more than the bodies pressed against him. The dank odor of sweat and garbage assaulted him. He tried to breathe slowly through his mouth, but that only made him feel like he was eating the foul odor, and it made his stomach cartwheel. At least two others had already vomited on themselves causing others to push away and create a mass movement of the group.

Gerardo looked down at his watch. A Timex Expedition. He lit up the face with the push of a button and couldn't help but laugh at the inexpensive watch on his wrist. He could remember only months ago when he paraded around town with his Rolex Submariner. A ridiculous gift to himself from his former life on the dark side. He sold the watch to make the crossing rather than risk drawing attention or getting robbed. It now seemed tragic that he spent more on the watch than most of these crossers would make in two years of back-breaking labor.

They had been driving for an hour. From an open screw hole on the side panel of the truck, Gerardo could see passing rocks and yucca. They were on a paved road, but it was not a freeway. From what he was told when he paid the coyote *jefe*, they would be picked up on the U.S. side by smaller passenger cars.

The truck began to slow, and it was as if the entire group could sense the journey in the heat and sweat trap was about to end. People pushed against each other to get a view through any of the small drill holes in the truck panel. From what Gerardo could tell, they were not near any commercial establishments. It looked slightly less foreboding than the area they had just left.

As the truck came to a stop, the anticipation of soon being released from the compartment was overwhelming. Strangers in the truck exchanged reassuring glances and fumbled for their possessions. Gerardo could hear the driver's side door shut and then the passenger side. He heard the distinct sound of two sets of footprints trail away from the truck.

Twenty. Thirty yards, he thought to himself. In the distance, Gerardo could make out the sound of an approaching vehicle. Straining to look sideways through the screw hole, Gerardo could barely make out the tailgate of a blue pickup. Then, in less than a few seconds, the doors of that truck opened and were shut again. The truck lurched out of his view. Gerardo could hear the truck idling and then that sound was gone.

The movement of bodies in the delivery truck had ceased, and the dead silence seemed to last for minutes.

"*Ay, Dios mío*," the old lady in the thick wool dress said, fright in her voice. "They have left us."

The others began to mutter that the old lady was right, they had been abandoned. How long would they be here, someone asked. Questions gave rise to a minor level of panic. Others said this was all part of the plan, they would be back.

Gerardo kept his thoughts to himself, but he kept looking at his watch. Thirty minutes had now passed and no action outside the truck. At sixty minutes the air was humid and thick, and the smell of sweat and fear penetrated every pore of his body. At ninety minutes women began to sob, and a few men began to speak openly about having been left purposely to die. After all, one man said, they had already paid. Gerardo began to think about the actions of the smugglers. He recalled that they did their best to keep everyone from looking at the children, but it was impossible for the crossers not to notice them. They were essentially witnesses to the trafficking of children. At two hours, Gerardo had to accept the reality that the smugglers had no intention of returning.

He was not going to die this way. Gerardo had done many things for which he deserved to die. But he hadn't been shot, no one had knifed him, and he'd even survived when a rival cartel threw him into a bear cage. Getting stuffed into the false compartment of a Chinese food delivery truck with a bunch of other poor immigrants was not the way he was leaving this earth.

"Listen up," Gerardo said to the fifteen or so men in the truck. "We need to do something to get out of here before we all start dying."

No one said anything, but there was a collective nod of agreement.

TWENTY-ONE

"How do we know we are not carrying a load of coke or meth?" Chino asked as he circled the trailer.

"What difference would it make?" Chance said as he dropped to the ground to get a look under the trailer.

"About twenty years in federal prison," Drew said. He was more concerned about where they were, exposed during the daylight, and the need to start moving.

Drew continued around the trailer.

"Fuck this!" he yelled. Drew opened the pickup driver's door and removed the keys from the ignition and walked to the rear of the trailer. Only one key and the truck remote on the chain. Drew used the key to unlock the padlock on the trailer door. Chino and Chance moved in behind Drew.

Drew removed the lock and pulled the door up from the handle at the base. It slid up easily. The inside of the trailer was clean. This was a problem. An off-road light buggy was strapped down inside and secured by rubber ties. The tires and the undercarriage had dried mud and the compartment smelled of gasoline. There was a large rolling tool stand secured in the corner, and four tires were bolted to the side of the trailer. Three red plastic twenty-gallon gasoline containers were strapped to the rear end of the trailer. Two helmets, multiple sets of gloves and what looked like jumpsuits were piled on top of each other in a mesh wire can in the corner. The suits were clean, and the gloves were new. Someone had gone through a lot of effort to make this trailer look like it was legitimately carrying an off-road racing vehicle. But something was wrong.

"Chino . . ." Drew said.

"Yeah. I know," Chino peered around the trailer.

"What's up? What's the problem?" Chance said, although he must have seen the problem.

"Too fucking clean, fat boy," Drew said without looking at Chance.

"If you are racing in the desert or mountains, you would expect the walls and the floors to be dirty. This thing is clean enough to eat off," Chino said. He ran the palm of his hand across the floor of the trailer.

"All right then," Drew said and turned to Chance and Chino. "Who has to piss?"

There was no need to explain things further. Drew and Chino turned and began to urinate into the dirt. The dusty red dirt was so dry that the urine streams kicked up their own little dust storm. When the two had finished, Chance stepped in with his foot to move the liquid around. All thee stomped their feet in the wet dirt and then walked around inside the trailer. Drew made sure that they simulated movements consistent with loading the vehicle, strapping the equipment down and securing other items. Chino rolled the jumpsuits through dirt and liquids inside the trailer. When they were finished, the interior had the appearance of three men having moved about the trailer performing ordinary tasks without concern for cleanliness.

"Be nice to have some empty Bud cans," Drew said absentmindedly.

"More like Tecate," Chance gave a nervous laugh.

"The thing is," Drew said as he stared at the floor of the trailer, "whatever or whoever we are carrying is below us right now. I don't hear any motor. That means that any cooling or air is going to be hooked up to the truck engine."

Drew followed his own line of reasoning.

"We need to move, and we need to move now."

Drew stepped out and yanked down the trailer door after Chance and Chino stepped out.

Drew got into the driver's seat of the pickup. Chance climbed into the rear of the cab, and Chino got into the passenger's seat.

"Anybody know anything about off-road racing?" Drew asked while looking straight down the long desert road.

Chino reached down and pulled out a cellphone from inside his high top.

"I will in a few minutes."

Drew affixed the yellow sticky note to the dashboard. The note had an address for a placed called the Rainbow Café. With only one way to go and one road, there was no need for GPS.

TWENTY-TWO

Panic was starting to seep into the pores of every person inside the truck. As they realized they might have been purposely left inside the truck, the urgency of the predicament mounted. Everyone in Mexico had heard tales of *polleros* leaving their loads of crossers stranded to die in the desert. They left them for a number of reasons, but at this moment, the reason didn't matter.

Women began to cry, which bothered Gerardo, but the bigger problem was he could see terror beginning to creep into the faces of the men. Panic caused men to do stupid things. Panic caused deadly stampedes at soccer matches and nightclubs. Gerardo knew he had to act. He knew he would have to assert himself or things would fall apart.

"*Cálmense todos!* Quiet!" Gerardo shouted with the authority of the law enforcement officer he once was.

At that instant, all movement and noise in the truck ceased except for some muffled sobbing from a few of the older women. Gerardo made a quick survey of the others in the compartment. There were eleven other men, not counting the man who looked to be in his seventies, and eight women.

"Everybody move back from the wall," he said.

The group was confined in a compartment about five feet wide. Gerardo began rapping a knuckle against the thick plywood looking for a soft spot. The wall seemed as solid as concrete. He half-joked to himself about leaving it to Mexicans to build a fortress of a false compartment. The others stayed silent and watched Gerardo contemplate the situation.

In the far right corner, about eight feet up, Gerardo noticed a smaller wooden compartment, about three by three feet. This had to be the air conditioning unit for the cargo. Gerardo remembered the coolness of the truck as they were led past the stacked parcels of foods with Asian writing on the labels. Of course, the cooled air was not directed into their impossibly cramped compartment, but now was not the time to note this to anyone in the oven where they were trapped.

Gerardo noticed moisture and drip condensation around the corners of the box and where the box contacted the compartment wall. This had to be the weakest part of the wall. Gerardo looked back over his shoulder and spotted a young man in his twenties, who appeared to be muscular and agile.

Gerardo motioned the young man over and grabbed him by the shoulders to turn his back away from the compartment wall. Gerardo pushed his back against the man and looked over his shoulder.

"We're going to climb," Gerardo said.

No words were necessary. The way up was self-explanatory. They would have to climb about seven or eight feet to reach the air conditioning unit. Gerardo reached behind him with his arms and locked them with the man behind him.

"*Listo*?" Gerardo asked him.

Still no words. Just a nod.

"You have a name?"

The young man nodded. "Chuey."

"Well, Chuey," Gerardo said as he looked at the desperate faces in the truck, "let's get out of here."

Gerardo started with his right leg pressed firm against the compartment wall and then lifted the left to make contact. He was surprised at how strong the pressure from Chuey's back was against his own. The raw strength of youth.

"One step at a time," Gerardo commanded. "On my count, one leg up. You start left; I start right."

No words from Chuey.

"Ready. Now step." Gerardo brought his right leg up.

"Now the next."

The pressure against his back was like a concrete wall. Chuey was built strong. His legs were churning and providing a lot of force.

"Next one." So it continued, and it was working. The two of them had risen about five feet, and Gerardo could see that he was within a few feet of the unit.

"Almost there," Gerardo said, mostly to himself.

Gerardo's legs were shaking, and his back felt like it had been hit by a truck. It looked like the last step would get him close enough to the unit to able to do some damage.

When he was level with the bottom of the unit, Gerardo was able to use a foot to tap enough to see that the plywood was wet and weaker than the rest of the wall. He shimmied both of his legs directly onto the wet area.

"Okay, Chuey," Gerardo said and tilted his head back and to the side so Chuey could hear him.

The faces of the others peered up at the two men suspended about eight feet above them.

"Do you want to die, Chuey?" Gerardo whispered.

"*Pues, no?*" Chuey answered as if it were a trick question.

"Well, we are all going to die in here unless we get through this wall, *comprendes?*"

Chuey did not respond, but Gerardo could feel Chuey's body tighten.

"I need you to push like your life depends on it. Because it does."

"*Órale,*" Gerardo shouted, "on three."

"*Uno,*" Chuey counted, "*dos, tres!*"

Gerardo could feel Chuey pushing against him with all his strength. Gerardo responded by flexing his legs against the wall with all his power and strength directed on the wettest spot.

At first, nothing was happening. Gerardo could hear Chuey breathing hard and could feel the sweat soaking through their shirts and on his back. A few long seconds went by, and then Gerardo could feel it. The wall was weakening and flexing.

"Almost there, Chuey."

The wall was now bowing, and Gerardo could make out the hint of a crack starting down from the unit. He scooted his left leg up against one side of the crack and started to bang it with the back of his heel. The crack began to lengthen.

"Okay," Gerardo said back to Chuey, "take one step back down."

Gerardo continued to kick at the crack and could now feel more flex in the wall. Gerardo and Chuey continued their crab crawl down the wall until they were only about five feet above the floor.

"*Está bien, Chuey,*" Gerardo said, "Let's let go and get down."

Releasing from Chuey was like getting out from under a car. Gerardo landed on his feet and reached his arms up high to straighten out his back.

"Okay," Gerardo said to all the men in the compartment, "we are all going to push this wall until it breaks."

A general nod of understanding came from most of the people, and several of the men positioned themselves along the base of the crack that Gerardo and Chuey had formed.

"On three," Gerardo said.

The men shuffled and planted their feet. Two of the taller men lifted themselves off the floor by placing their feet against the back of the compartment and climbing up the wall. The two positioned themselves above the crack about five feet off the ground.

The heat inside the compartment was unbearable, and every breath was thick with the smell of sweat and fear.

"*Uno, dos,*" Gerardo positioned his hands next to the crack, "*tres! Todos juntos!*"

At that moment the collective force of twenty trapped and frightened humans pushed against the wall. At first, nothing. Then, after what seemed like minutes, the wall began to creak and flex. Gerardo could see the crack grow larger and extend toward the floor. Gerardo motioned for Chuey to move with him to the side of the crack that was below the air conditioning compartment. From that position both of them pushed. Gerardo could feel the wall giving in.

"We are close," Gerardo yelled. "*Un poco más!*"

As soon as he said it, the wall made a loud cracking sound as the wood split. The bottom section Gerardo was pushing against became separated from the wall, and he pushed it through. He could see into the trailer area. He pushed the section forward, and it bent at about the level of his waist.

The others watched as Gerardo shimmied through the hole and disappeared. A few seconds later he popped his head back in through the hole.

"Chuey!" Gerardo motioned for him to come forward. "You help each person through, push the *viejitos* if you have to."

Gerardo made his way over the boxes of frozen Chinese goods to the rear door of the truck. He pulled slowly up on the handle, hoping to God that the door was not locked from the outside. The door slid easily, and Gerardo pulled it up.

The light from outside was blinding. It seemed as if a gigantic spotlight had been trained directly at his eyes. Gerardo could make out the mountains in the distance, but he had to look down to the ground to adjust his eyes. Turning back to the truck, he could see the others emerging like prisoners released from an underground bunker. Some held their hands up over their eyes, others grabbed the shoulder of the person in front of them to be led away.

Now that he was out, Gerardo realized he had to figure out what to do next. Wandering about the desert brush with twenty beaten down travelers in the hot sun did not seem like a good idea. The large number of people in broad daylight was guaranteed to get noticed. Gerardo also knew the group would look to him to lead them.

Gerardo looked up at the sun with his right-hand fingers spread to protect his eyes. He could guess it was near noon. He looked around. About a quarter mile away he could see a road. No traffic so it could not be a freeway. Behind him and to the front end of the truck, the land began to rise toward the scrub-pocked mountains.

As much as he wanted to help these poor people, Gerardo knew that with them he would have no chance of making it out of the desert alive and without being detected by *la migra*, or worse, the traffickers. Not my problem, he told himself. Without looking back at the group, he began to run toward the mountains and away from the truck. At first, he began to trot slowly away, but then he accelerated for a good two hundred yards. He traversed through the cactus and scrub so others would not follow. After being stuffed inside the truck for so long, the rush of fresh hot air filling his lungs was a pleasant experience. It seemed to give him more energy to run. After a good sixty seconds, Gerardo dropped to the ground behind a fallen mesquite tree. He lay on his back for a few minutes, not daring to look back at the truck for fear the others were behind him.

Staring up the blazingly blue sky, he could feel the sun heat up his skin and knew he should get to some shade. Gerardo remained in the sun for a few moments, his mind playing back the events that had led to him lying in the dirt again, this time somewhere in the backcountry of San Diego.

God damn dirt. Gerardo laughed to himself and rolled under the shade of some shrubs to wait for the night.

TWENTY-THREE

The three drove in complete silence as if there had been some agreement that they all sit quietly and contemplate the gravity of the situation. There was nothing to say, Drew thought. All of them had made the jump from citizen to criminal when they drove the truck and rig away. More importantly, they had all chosen not to inquire as to what they were carrying.

Mile after mile. Minute after minute. Silence.

Thoughts raced through Drew's mind. He thought of his children, about Katie. He thought of being away from them. He thought of prison. He did his best to shake those thoughts, but the one thing he couldn't keep out of his head was what was in the trailer. Could he be transporting a group of Islamic terrorists? A WMD? Did he want to go down in history as the guy who let this happen?

"Fuck no," Drew said out loud and braked hard to pull the truck and trailer over. The truck started to skid, and the trailer fishtailed. Drew regained control of the truck and pulled off in a dirt clearing partially blocked by some leafy desert ironwood trees.

Chance hit his head on the passenger side window. "What the fuck, Drew!"

The truck came to a stop and idled on the side of the roadway.

Drew sat silent for a moment. Chance and Chino waited for him to speak.

"I need to know," Drew finally said without looking at either of them.

"Wait a minute," Chance said.

Drew took off his sweat-wrung ball cap, tossed it onto the dash and ran his fingers through his hair. He turned square to Chino and looked back to Chance.

"Look," Drew said, with an eye out for traffic coming up from behind them. "The way I see it is that we are in the shit."

"But we don't know . . ." Chance blurted out before Drew's gaze stopped him dead.

"I don't give a shit if these guys are major Mexican badasses. I'm not going another foot until I know what we are carrying."

"Drew," Chino said more as a plea, "they have our names and home addresses, they can reach our families."

"Thing is Chino, we don't know if we are carrying a couple of poor-ass Mexicans or a nuke. Right now, we still have a chance."

A car was coming up behind so Drew kept eye contact as the car passed by them. It was a newer pickup, not unusual for this area. Two dark-skinned men, both wearing ball caps. Again, not unusual. Maybe he was paranoid, but he thought the driver of the vehicle slowed a little as he passed the truck. Drew turned his attention to Chino and Chance.

"If it's bad," Drew continued, "we can walk away. We can take our chances with these assholes, but we won't be fucking ourselves in the process."

"Or we could just do the drop, collect our money and never see each other again," Chance said almost in a whisper. "The way I see it is that we are all in right now. This thing has started, and it's not going to stop so we might as well get paid for the risk."

"Fat boy's got a point," Chino said.

"Fuck that shit," Drew said, looking back again for traffic. "If this is coke, meth, or heroin, we are looking at ten years minimum, and it could be something way worse."

"You're saying that if this trailer is loaded with anything but Mexicans we are walking away?" Chance asked.

"Damn straight!"

The three sat silent for a few seconds. Drew had his window half cranked, and the only sound was that of wind blowing through the brush around them.

"Well, I'm with you Drew," Chino said almost in resignation, "but if we are going to do anything, we need to do it now instead of sitting out here with our dicks in our hand."

"Copy that," Drew said as he opened his door and stepped out of the truck.

Drew made his way to the trailer, and the others got out and followed him.

As much as they tried to dirty up the trailer to make it look used, it appeared suspiciously new. As he approached the white trailer with bright red racing strips, Drew thought it would certainly draw attention when compared to the miles of dirty, desert scrub around them.

Drew walked around to the back of the trailer and opened the rear sliding door. All three peered in.

"We need to find the compartment door," Drew said, moving his hand around the trailer floor.

Chino stepped into the trailer and made his way to the back. He stopped in the middle where an engine winch was mounted to the floor. The winch was sitting on top of a metal plate also bolted to the trailer floor. There was something about the position of the bolts that looked out of place. Chino could not put his finger on it, but something was off. He reached down to the base of the winch and pulled it back and forth. The floor plate of the base moved right to left a few centimeters.

"Drew," Chino said, looking back toward the others, "looks like I may have something here."

Drew and Chance stepped farther into the trailer. Drew reached down to the base of the winch. Four bolts held the winch in place, but with a closer look, he could tell three of the bolts were soldered shut. Only one bolt looked like it could be tightened or loosened. Drew stood up and looked around the trailer.

"Chino," he said, "hand me the Channellock hanging behind you."

Chino reached for the brand new, red rubber-gripped pliers behind him and handed them to Drew handles first. Drew went to work loosening the only bolt that looked functional. With some effort, the bolt head began to move. As it loosened, Drew could feel this was a particularly long bolt holding the winch in place. He got to the point where the bolt was completely loose, dropped the pliers, and started to finish the loosening with his fingers. The bolt separated from the plate, and Drew could see there was another plate beneath the base of the winch about eighteen by eighteen inches square.

"Give me a hand," Drew said and motioned for the other two to come forward.

Chance and Chino grabbed hold of the winch and started to lift it up, and, with a slight tug, it separated from the floor of the trailer. Drew looked down at the plate. Four more large bolts. These were not as securely fastened, and Drew made quick work of loosening and removing three of them. Drew could feel the plate had loosened enough for him to pull it up a bit and rotate it on the still attached bolt.

Chance and Chino moved closer to see what Drew was doing and to get a better view of the cargo in which they had just invested their lives. Drew pushed the plate to the far right and could see through the opening. He could see yellow-green foam loosely packed like insulation. Drew looked up to Chino who gave him a silent nod to pull up the foam. Drew reached down with his right hand and pulled away about six inches of the material.

"Jesus Christ!" Drew yelled as he recoiled.

In the instant after he pulled back the foam, Drew saw the unmistakable face of a very young and very frightened little girl. Her face was covered with residue of the foam, and she was dripping wet with sweat and tears.

As Drew turned to say something to Chino, he heard a car pull up and stop near the front of the trailer. Chance and Chino also heard it, and the three of them stood in stunned silence for a few seconds until Chance turned to move toward the entryway. Drew could see Chance reach the entrance and, with his body still inside the trailer, he craned his head outside to see what was there.

Drew reached back and grabbed the large pliers he had been using and looked to Chino hoping he might try to find something to arm himself with. Just then, he saw Chance retreating from the trailer gate. He also saw the gun barrel that was directing him.

TWENTY-FOUR

Gerardo had been lying under the shade of the mesquite shrub for a few hours. He did not want to risk walking in the open terrain in daylight. He knew the Border Patrol had helicopters and patrols in the area. He also knew that the self-styled "Border Keepers" vigilantes roamed the backcountry looking for crossers. Gerardo could see dusk approaching. The temperature was dropping, and it had been hours since he last saw the group from the truck. He rose slowly to avoid attention, and below him, all he saw was the truck still parked along the dirt road. Gerardo could also make out the mass of footprints in the dirt as they headed due west. That was certainly the way he needed to go, but he had to figure out another route since the large group would no doubt attract the attention of the Border Patrol. The hilltop he was standing on rose a few hundred feet from the desert floor. He could see the faint glow of lights to the north. Gerardo figured it must be a gas station. If he could make it there, he could flag down a ride or stow away on a truck.

He made his way down the hillside, figuring there might be some food or water he might be able to salvage from the truck. That is, if it had not been pillaged already by the others.

As he approached the truck, he noticed the foul stench of the now hot seafood that had served as the cover of legitimate cargo. Nothing in the storage area could be used. He searched every conceivable hiding place in the cab for a set of keys to start the truck. No luck. The glove compartment yielded a pack of cigarettes with three remaining, a flashlight, a screwdriver and a pair of pliers. He left the cigarettes and put the screwdriver and pliers in his back pocket. One last place to look, behind the seats. He ran the flat of his palm down the backside of the driver's seat and found nothing. Moving to the passenger's side, he once again ran his palm down the back until it stopped on something hard. He knew the feel of a handgun without needing to see it. He could tell it was a semi-auto just from what he could touch.

Gerardo pulled out the handgun. Glock nine-millimeter. These *polleros* and *narcos* had no imagination, he thought. Whatever guys were wearing or using in the movies is what they wanted. Popping the clip, he found it fully loaded.

One never knows, he thought. Better safe than shot in the back of the head and left in this *pinche* desert. He tucked the weapon between his belt and waist.

Off in the distance, he could see low-flying Border Patrol helicopters with their piercing spotlight beams scanning the desert floor. At night it was also easier to see the headlights from the patrolling SUVs. Keeping an eye on the lights in the distance, he moved slowly through brush and found his way to a dry wash that showed signs of smuggler use in the past. The dry creek was littered with the telltale refuse of border crossers—empty water bottles, candy bar wrappers, discarded clothing. Given the popularity of this route, Gerardo knew he would have to work his way out and find something less traveled. After a few hundred yards, he saw a single path out of the creek bed and up the ridge that ran along the creek and in the direction of the lights.

When Gerardo made it to the top of the ridge, he could make out that the lights belonged to a service station and garage. He could also see that if he continued on the ridge, he would come within about a hundred yards of the station from an elevated position. From there he could watch in safety until he figured out what to do next.

TWENTY-FIVE

The hard plastic dug into Drew's flesh. They had their hands zip-tied from the front. Their legs were also bound by zip ties at the ankles. All three of them were in the bed of the pickup and had been ordered to stay down. The fat one rode in the truck bed and was watching over them with his gun in hand. It seemed like they had been driven about five miles in a relatively straight direction. Drew could see trees and other objects taller than the truck bed.

"Fuck. Fuck." Chance was starting to panic.

"What's our play, Drew?" Chino asked in a low voice.

"Don't know. I can't imagine that us finding human cargo in the vehicle that we thought we were supposed to be transporting human cargo would be such a big deal unless there was something special about this load."

"You said you saw a little girl. Are you sure?"

"Little girl, little boy. What does it matter?"

"Whatever they are, we are fucking dead unless we can figure something out," Chance said.

"You're right about that," Drew looked over to Chino and then to Chance. "We need to do whatever is necessary to survive."

Drew looked over at the man with the gun. He stayed perched on the wall of the pickup bed, keeping guard over them. Drew noticed the gunman's attention was directed at his associates. He could see them talking, but Drew guessed he was not concerned given their captivity and his knowledge of the likely outcome.

"Any ideas?" Chino asked.

"Working on it," Drew said as the truck slowed and came to a stop.

From the bed, Drew could make out the glow of lights. A commercial establishment. A truck stop, gas station. Something. He could hear the driver's door of the truck open and footsteps.

The fat man jumped out of the bed and walked forward. He could hear some muffled words in Spanish. The man with the mirrored glasses opened the bed of the pickup. He motioned for the fat one to get up and cut the ankle ties on all three.

"Up, you *pendejos*," the man yelled.

Standing outside the pickup, Drew could now see that the vehicle with the trailer had been following them and was now parked behind them. Drew assessed the threat level. Fucking high. Very fucking high. The three of them unarmed, zip tied at the wrists, versus two *narcos* holding Glock nines. *What is it with Glocks and criminals?* The more problematic of the two, Drew thought, was the cold hired gun with the mirrored sunglasses. Drew called him Sunglasses when he was talking to Chino as they left the first meeting. Drew knew he would be a problem the first time he saw him. Now Sunglasses stood pointing his gun at him in a very confident manner. Only at Drew and looking only at Drew.

For what seemed an eternity, no one said a word.

TWENTY-SIX

From atop the ridge, Gerardo watched it unfold. He saw the lights of the pickup moving along the road toward the service station and saw it stop a quarter mile short behind some trees. The truck hauled the trailer he had seen earlier. The one they loaded with the children, two by two. This was not good, he thought. Three men standing against the truck and two others pointing guns at them. He had seen this before, and it always ended badly for those not holding the guns.

He weighed his options. Do nothing, which meant three dead men. Gerardo did not know their story. Maybe they were part of the ring. Maybe they deserved what was coming. But the children were a different story. He knew they were not being smuggled in to be reunited with hard-working and caring families. He knew they were not being smuggled in to be adopted by well-meaning and loving people. No. He knew they were being brought in as prey. They were being brought in as playthings.

Gerardo watched the men who were being held captive. There was something about them. Their body language. He could tell at least two of them were surveying their predicament, looking for a move. No resignation visible in their posture. Gerardo had seen captured men executed before and, for the most part, they usually accepted their predicament. A consequence of the life they had chosen. These men were different. He couldn't be sure, especially in the dark, but it appeared that these soon-to-be executed men had been driving the truck and trailer. He did not need to get any closer to determine that the trailer was the object of dispute

Gerardo had the ability to affect fifteen lives. Do nothing and three men die and twelve children become victims. Do something and risk death or, at best, a lifetime of looking over his shoulder for the *narco* assassin they will send for him. In Culiacan, he had grown into a life in which he did nothing for anyone but himself. After he delivered his friend to Cicatriz to be murdered, Gerardo came to the agonizing realization he needed to change. He left his daughter with her mother in Monterrey, and there would be no way he would be able to see her again, at least in Mexico. Staying in Culiacan, on the other hand, would mean he would be responsible for more deaths, including his own, or worse, his family's.

Maybe this was the time for him to step up.

He realized the stress of watching had caused him to dig his fingers deep into the red clay dirt in which he was lying. The dirt encrusted his fingernails, and he wiped them off on his shirt.

"Dirt," he said to himself and smothered a laugh.

Gerardo chambered a round in the Glock and made his way down the side of the ridge on his stomach.

TWENTY-SEVEN

Drew kept his eyes on the man with the mirrored glasses, whose gun was not pointed at them directly. The other man, the fat one, had his firearm pointed directly at them, arm outstretched, elbow locked. Drew knew, of course, the one with the glasses held the gun barrel down in front of him to reduce the strain and fatigue on his arm, but he had no doubt this man could efficiently aim and fire the weapon at any time. The fact that the three of them were bound and had nowhere to run most likely gave him the confidence to relax his arm. This one had some training. Military, probably not. Law enforcement, most likely.

They stood silently for a long minute. Funny, Drew thought, it was just like the movies, he could hear a pack of coyotes howling off in the distance. The wind was also blowing hard and loud, swirling dust, and pushing dead brush.

Sunglasses reached for his cellphone and started to talk to someone in Spanish. The fat one continued to point his gun at the three, and it was clear to Drew that his arms were starting to tire. Sunglasses tucked his weapon into his front waistband as he spoke on the phone. Three targets for the fat man, ten feet or so between them. Drew figured he could cover the distance in about two seconds with the element of surprise. Sunglasses would react quickly and probably be able to hit one or two of them before he could get the weapon out of tub of lard's hands. Drew knew he would have to struggle, but it would take no more than two seconds to disable him. At the same time, Drew had to account for the fact that his hands were bound. He would have to get a grip of the firearm and not let go. He decided the better plan was to go for Sunglasses first. He was the threat. Drew would have to take him out. It would take an extraordinary combination of timing and luck to neutralize Sunglasses before being wounded or killed. Still, Drew was not going to fool himself into thinking there was any way out of this that did not include their execution. Nothing to lose.

"Need you to move with me when it's on," Drew whispered as he turned his face to the ground. "You mark the fat man."

Chino said nothing. No need to. Drew knew Chino would follow him into any fight. At present, there was only one fight, and it was right in front of them.

"*Quieto, pendejos!*" yelled sunglasses as he looked up from the phone.

Drew could not see behind the mirrored glasses but he was dead certain the eyes were trained on him. Sunglasses went back to speaking on the phone, but he didn't turn away from the trio. Drew saw the fat one's arm drop lower. He could also see thick beads of sweat running down the sides of his chunky face. If there ever were a time, it would be now. Drew readied himself and pulled his right foot back a few inches to start his run. As he did, Sunglasses stopped talking and reached for the gun in his waistband. Walking toward them now with the Glock pointed and ready, Drew knew his opportunity had passed.

He stopped within two feet of Drew and then walked slowly sideways across the three and stopped in front of Chance. Drew knew at that instant Sunglasses had determined that Chance was the weak link. Drew looked over at Chance and could see his hands were trembling by his side.

"You *putos* had one job," Sunglasses said, pointing the gun barrel a few inches away from Chance's forehead, "and you fucked it up."

The fat one took a few steps closer to Drew and pointed his gun at the group. Drew could tell this guy had no formal training in firearms. He surmised his ability to hit a target would decrease by every inch of separation. The Glock he was holding was accurate at close range but required some degree of skill, at the six or seven feet he was standing from the group, to hit a moving target.

For a few long seconds, the man in the mirrored glasses said nothing as he pulled his face closer to Chance. The gun barrel now directly against Chance's forehead. Drew could see the reflection of Chance's face in the glasses. He was tearing up. Chance was scared.

Drew's heartbeat was racing. *Damn it! Two tours in combat in some foreign country and now he was going to die on some dirt road in his own backyard. Fuck that.* He was certain now that he had to rush Sunglasses. He was the most lethal. Drew would have to rely on the fat one's lack of training and Chino's reflexes to rush him. Just as he was finishing the thought, Sunglasses pulled the gun away from Chance's forehead and brought the butt of the gun backhanded against Chance's head. Chance went down to the ground, and Sunglasses continued to strike him with the metal part of the barrel. The thud of metal on a skull was something that Drew was all too familiar with in war. Blood flew from the weapon every time Sunglasses pulled back to deliver another blow. Drew was sure the man was going to beat Chance to death.

Drew looked over at the fat one, who had his attention on his partner beating Chance. Now or never. Now, or they would all be dead.

TWENTY-EIGHT

Gerardo watched the beating from behind a set of boulders. After silently sliding down the hill on his stomach, he moved deliberately so he would not cause any audible disturbance. His weapon was tucked behind his back in his waistband. He could identify the man with the sunglasses as the leader and recognized the fat one from crossing the prior evening. He was the one he saw loading the children into the trailer. He could see the one with the sunglasses pointing a gun at the man on his knees wearing a basketball jersey. Gerardo also noticed that the one to his right, who had an ex-military look to him, was about to make a move. He could see the man assessing the two who were holding guns. It was a bad situation for the gringos lined up in the dirt. Gerardo had seen it all before. A bullet to the head and three bodies lying in the red clay dirt to rot.

It wasn't his problem. He kept trying to convince himself of that, but he couldn't stop thinking about the children packed away in the trailer. No, this was it. Maybe this was his chance. Maybe he could reclaim just a bit of his soul.

From his position about twenty yards away, Gerardo could see the one with sunglasses begin to pistol whip one of the men. He had to make his move now because this was the beginning of the end for the three men. Gerardo knew this man would beat the American to death for his pleasure and then execute the other two. He knew he would have to come out shooting. In real life, no one holding a gun ever put his hands up when approached by someone else with a gun.

Gerardo knew he had to take out the fat one first and then start firing at the one in sunglasses. He didn't think the fat one could hit him from that distance because of the way he held the gun, too careless.

This was his chance, his only chance, if he was going to save them. It was time to get in the game.

Gerardo pulled the weapon out from his waistband. He checked the chamber on the Glock and rose to his feet in a crouch.

TWENTY-NINE

After the first blow against his skull, Chance crumpled to the ground. After about the third sickening thud, Drew knew he had to act. As the man brought the gun up to begin another blow, Drew began his charge. His physical training in the Marines covered a whole range of physical activities but, in the tiniest sliver of his mind, he remembered his drill instructor screaming at them during wind sprints, "Acceleration will save your life, fuckheads!" At the time, that did not seem to make a lot of sense. Now he was going to put it to the test.

Drew lunged and covered the ten feet before Sunglasses could bring the gun barrel back down on Chance's skull. Drew pulled off a textbook tackle that took them both to the ground and left Sunglasses gasping for air but struggling with Drew, who had a good grip of the hand that was holding the gun. He could feel the man's fingernails digging into his wrist, trying to free the hand. The man's grip on the gun loosened, and it spilled to the ground. The dirt they were wrestling in was dusty and dry, and Drew could taste the earth in his throat. Drew rammed his forearm under the man's chin and started pressuring down on the windpipe as hard as he could.

Then he heard a gunshot. Then another.

Sunglasses stopped struggling and looked in the direction of the shots. Drew stayed on top of him with his forearm still pressing down hard on his throat, but he risked a look to see if Chino had been hit. He was not expecting to see another man holding a gun.

He could see Chino was still standing and that Chance was lying in the dirt still bleeding from his head and face. The man, a Latino wearing a baseball cap, had dirt caked over the front of his shirt and thighs of his jeans. He stood over the fat one, reached down, picked the gun out of the fat man's hand, and tucked it into the back of his waistband. Fat boy was not moving, and he was bleeding from a large hole in his chest. The man pointed the gun at Drew and walked toward him. He kicked the gun Sunglasses had been holding, and it slid a good ten feet away from Drew. The man kept his gun pointed at Drew and Sunglasses and went over to pick up the other weapon. After retrieving it, he gestured for Drew to get off Sunglasses and move back to where Chance and Chino were standing.

Drew got up and backed slowly to a place near Chino. He could not assess the risk. This man didn't seem aligned with the ones who were about to kill him and his companions. *Your enemy's enemy is your friend.* Chino looked equally confused.

The man kept his full attention on Sunglasses, who was now sitting up in the dirt. Drew noticed that during the takedown and struggle, the man had not lost his sunglasses.

"*Te conozco, pendejo,*" Sunglasses said in an accusatory tone.

"Shut up, *cabrón!*" the man said, the gun still pointed down.

The man looked at Drew and Chino. He tossed one of the guns, a Sig Sauer nine-millimeter, to where Chance was lying and reached back into his waistband and tossed the other gun by Drew's feet.

Drew knew he did this to show he was no threat to them.

"*Investigador Rios,*" Sunglasses said in a sarcastic tone. "*Tú sabes que estás chingado, no?*"

Drew didn't understand much Spanish but he figured the man with the gun was a police officer, and the people for whom Sunglasses worked knew him, and the man was most definitely fucked.

Chance was still moaning but managed to rise slowly to his feet with the gun in his hand. The man looked over at the three of them.

"You gringos okay?"

"Looks like it," Drew said as he surveyed the fallout from the scuffle. "Thanks for the help."

"All of you are fucked," Sunglasses said with a bit of a laugh at the end.

"No, no, no," Chance said as he approached Sunglasses. The beating had opened a three-inch gash on his forehead, and there was blood all over the front of his jersey. In his zip-tied hands, Chance had the Sig Sauer. He stopped in front of Sunglasses, who was sitting up in the dirt. "You are fucked," he said, spitting blood.

Chance quickly leveled the gun at Sunglasses' head and fired.

Drew had seen plenty of death while deployed, but this was different. He was not expecting this doughy gangster wanna-be to turn cold assassin. The blast sent half of Sunglasses' skull ten feet from his body with a trail that sprayed the dry dirt with the red-black blood. The body lay sprawled out across the dirt on its back. The sunglasses were finally off the face, lying haphazardly in bloody clumps of brain and dirt.

"Holy shit!" Chino said, standing open-mouthed over the body.

Chance said nothing and stood still, panting like he had just finished a run and holding the gun loosely in his right hand. He continued to spit and cough up blood.

"Holy shit!" Chino repeated. He had not moved.

Drew was equally shocked by the deliberate violence. He looked over at the man who had come to their aid.

Gerardo remained rigid after the execution.

Seconds passed between the men.

Drew broke the silence.

"So, who the hell are you?" Drew took a moment to take in the bloody scene again. "And, by the way, thanks a lot for saving our ass."

Gerardo remained mute for a moment, but not because of the violent nature of the encounter. He was running through his head what Sunglasses had said to him. They knew him, and he was fucked.

"Gerardo," he said, still contemplating the gravity of the situation. "Gerardo Rios."

Chance backed away from the body and stood to the right of Chino, who could not take his eyes off the body.

"Fuck that dude," Chance said as he spit blood in his general direction.

Sunglasses lay face up, but with his hips slightly turned so that his belt buckle almost touched the dirt. As Gerardo moved around the body, he noticed something inside the dead man's jeans pocket. He pushed the hip back with his foot. Even though it was concealed in the pocket, a phone could be discerned.

"*Puta madre!*" Gerardo said in a low whisper.

He reached into the pocket and retrieved the phone. Drew took a step closer to look. The screen was black, and Gerardo held out hope the phone was turned off. He pushed the power button, and the all-too-familiar display of lights and caller ID appeared. The ID read Numero Uno. Gerardo held the phone to his ear. Still connected. No sound on the other end.

Sunglasses had been on the phone when the violence began. They were on their way.

"We've got to bounce, now!" Drew shouted to Chino and Chance.

Gerardo dropped the phone on the ground and crushed it with the heel of his boot. He picked it back up and put the phone in his pocket.

"I will dump this somewhere down the road," Gerardo said as he walked to the trailer.

"Chino," Drew's voice was slow and deliberate, "you drive the trailer with Chance."

"Copy that."

"Rios, right?" Drew asked.

"Gerardo Rios, yes."

"You ride in the back of the . . ." Drew started to say.

"You know what you are carrying?" Gerardo interrupted.

Drew nodded and motioned for Gerardo to make his way to the back of the trailer.

"You ride inside the trailer and pull them out to make sure they are okay," Drew said, pointing to the trailer door and then to Chino. "I will take the *narco* truck, and you follow behind."

Chance was still standing over the body of the man with sunglasses.

"Chance," Chino yelled, "we've got to move!"

Chance, bleeding from the head and mouth, trotted back to the truck. Chino was inside rummaging through the console for the keys. He found them on the floorboard.

"Drew," Chino said, popping his head out of the driver's side window, "where are we going?"

He had no idea. Drew knew a posse of gunmen was on its way. He knew they had heard the gunfire. He knew there could be no good end to this.

"We need to get out of here and get word to our families to get to safety."

"Copy that," Chino popped his head back into the truck and started the engine. Gerardo climbed into the trailer and pulled the door down behind him.

Drew walked back to the *narco* truck. He stopped by the body to search for anything valuable to him. He patted Sunglasses for weapons and found a .380 auto tucked into his snakeskin boot and a butterfly knife in his front pocket. Drew grabbed the man's wallet and tucked it into his back pocket. As he stepped away from the body, Drew heard a crunch. He looked down and saw that he stepped on the sunglasses that now lay flat in the dirt, both lenses shattered but still held within the frame.

"Fuck you, asshole," Drew whispered to himself.

He climbed into the jacked-up *narco* four-by-four and started the engine. Loud ranchero music immediately blared through speakers. Drew slammed his palm against the radio knobs and killed the sound. He drove the pickup in front of the trailer and motioned with his arm out the window for Chino to follow.

This was bad. Very fucking bad. He put the truck in gear and drove off.

THIRTY

Inside the trailer, the hum and grind of the truck engine were deafening to Gerardo. He could see the area by the winch that looked like the access panel to the compartment. He began to work off the base plate of the engine lift. The plate was already loose, and he had an easy time rotating it away. He knew what he was going to see, but he wasn't quite ready for the reality. The face of a young girl peered up at him covered in sweat and foam insulation. Her expression was blank, yet she was clearly in distress. He reached down and pushed the almost black hair away from her face.

"*Todo está bien,*" he told her in a reassuring tone.

The girl did not respond, and he could now see her pupils were dilated, and her eyes were glassy. She had been drugged, no doubt making the transportation easier and, more importantly, quiet. Gerardo reached down under her arms and pulled her up carefully. As he did, he was able to see the line of children lying next to her in a row. They were still bound two by two with slack between the pairs. All of them not moving. Awake yet lifeless eyes.

He sat the first girl up against the side of the trailer and then reached in for the second child. A boy, about seven years old wearing tiny cowboy boots. He was also groggy from the drugs. After placing him next to the girl, Gerardo climbed down into the compartment so he could reach the others. It was dark and hot. The air was thick with the smell of sweat. The smell of urine. One or more of the children must have urinated in their clothes. Out of necessity, maybe out of fear. There was just enough room for Gerardo to crawl on his stomach to reach the other children. He slowly pulled them out one by one being careful with the rope. After he placed the last child sitting against the trailer wall, he looked around him. Twelve small children propped up against the side of the trailer, limp from drugs and half awake. They reminded him of the puppets he used to see hanging from the stalls in the *mercado* when he was young.

He considered his situation., and it wasn't good. He was in the back of a trailer with twelve drugged children. They could be stopped by the Border Patrol, and he would most definitely end up in prison. In prison, he would not be safe because Caritas and his associates could easily reach him. In addition, they had killed two men. The law would want to hold them responsible, and Caritas would want to kill them. That prospect was most sobering. Very few things had any value to the narcos and *polleros*. Honor, at least their twisted version of it, mattered most. You could not kill one of theirs and not suffer the consequences. Someone would have to pay. Friend or family, it didn't matter to them. Gerardo was in this now, and he would have to deal with the consequences of his decision to come to the aid of these gringos and the children.

He knew what had to happen. He knew what was to come all too well since he had been part of it in the past. It would end in the dirt. Gerardo pulled the Glock out of his waistband and ejected the clip. Examining it, he could see that he had six rounds left. Not enough. Not nearly enough.

THIRTY-ONE

"Fuck. Fuck. Fuck!" Drew was nearly shouting as he drove the truck down the dusty road.

This was a bad idea to start with, and it was now a hell of a lot worse. Caritas and his men knew who they were. They had their identifications, home addresses. They would be coming for them. Katie and the boys were with her parents for the weekend, so he had a little time. He didn't know Chino's situation and less about Chance. The whole thing was FUBAR, not to mention the legal implications of the outright execution by Chance. Thoughts raced through Drew's mind. Fuck. DNA left at the scene with the bodies? Fingerprints left somewhere? Watching too much CSI can screw with your head. At least, he thought, they had crushed the phone and the GPS locator in it. Then he noticed the edge of a metal box on the floor of the passenger's side, partially exposed from under the seat. He reached down and slid the box out. The box was dark green, almost black, with a flashing green light.

"Fuck!" Drew slammed on the brakes, bringing the truck to a skid.

The truck and trailer that Chino was driving also skidded to a stop.

Drew got out of the truck Sunglasses and his fat companion had been driving and started walking toward the trailer hitched to the other truck.

Chino leaned out the driver's window of the pickup doing the hauling.

"What's up, Drew."

"GPS! GPS!" Drew said, not even looking at Chino. He threw himself on the dirt and rolled under the trailer. It didn't take long to find it. Of course, these traffickers would have a GPS locator on their vehicles. The cargo was valuable, and the vehicles were spread out all over the San Diego backcountry.

Drew rolled back out from under the trailer. Chino, Chance, and Gerardo had all got out of the vehicles and were standing to the side of the trailer.

"GPS, boys," Drew said as he lifted himself from the ground. "Just found the locator box in the truck. They know where we are, and you can bet they're coming."

Chino moved forward in a crouch to get a look at the device.

"Then we need to smash that shit up."

"Wait," Gerardo had come out from behind the trailer. "They don't know that we know."

Drew followed the thought.

"He's right. Knowledge is power at this point."

Gerardo put his right hand over the butt of the handgun sticking out from his waistband.

"Right now, we know men are coming to kill us. They know who we are and where we live. I can tell you that they will not stop. They cannot stop because it is a matter of pride and business. They cannot allow this to happen. I have six rounds that are going to have to count. Six less men to come after me or visit my family and friends."

Chance, still bloody and shaken, pulled out his gun to check the clip.

"He's right," Chance said as he eyed the clip and clicked it back into the handle. "We need to deal with this now. I have seven rounds left."

Drew knew they were right, but they would have to take it one step further.

"We need to get back to Caritas," he said. He had already checked his weapon. "I've got ten rounds left."

"I have seven," Chino said, reloading the clip.

"That makes thirty rounds between us," Drew said and looked back down the road for any sign of vehicles. "We need to draw them into a position of advantage for us."

"Fuck yes!" Chance said, still pumped from an adrenaline rush. "We need to waste these fuckers."

Gerardo looked over to Drew because he could see who was in charge of the group and who was capable of making rational decisions.

"We cannot kill them all," Gerardo said.

"Why the fuck not?" Chance said, anger in his voice.

"We need to question at least one of them. We need to find out where Caritas is at and get to him," Gerardo said. He could see they understood what he was driving at. "This will never end unless we put an end to it."

"He's got a point," Drew brushed the dirt off the back of his jeans, "problem is what to do with the kids."

"How many are there?" Chino asked Gerardo.

"Twelve, six boys, six girls all between six and eight years old, and all of them have been drugged."

"Can they walk?" Drew asked.

"Not anytime soon."

"So we stand our ground and ambush these fuckers!" Chino said, looking to Drew for support.

"Then what do we do with these drugged-out kids?" Drew asked.

"Nothing," Gerardo said firmly. "We leave them in the trailer."

"We can't do—" Drew started to say.

"We have the truck and GPS locator, correct?" Gerardo interrupted.

"Yes, we do."

"Then we let them take the trailer, and we follow with the tracker," Gerardo said, still looking down the road for signs of vehicles. "It is too late in the day for them to make the drop, so they will have to go back to their home base."

Drew began to understand the plan.

"Right," he said, "we take the fight to them under the cover of dark."

"What about the kids?" Chino asked.

"They are a valuable cargo to them," Gerardo answered. "No harm will come to them until . . ."

". . . they get to the sick fucks who bought them," Chance finished.

"Okay," Drew said. "Let's check on these kids and make sure they are all right before we leave them here."

"The drugs have made them very sleepy," Gerardo said as he pulled the trailer door open. "Their heart rate is down, and even though it can't be good for them, they won't be in any sort of pain for a few more hours."

Drew and Chino stepped up into the trailer. The children were in the same positions where Gerardo left them, all propped up against the inside walls of the trailer. Only two were somewhat conscious. The others were all out, breathing but lifeless.

"Motherfuckers," Chino looked over to Drew.

Drew, standing next to him, could not say a thing.

"We've got to get out of here and plan our move," Chance said.

"Gordito's right," Gerardo said with a sense of urgency. "We are running out of time."

Chance nodded in agreement but with the slight annoyance he just been called chubby.

Drew looked over at the man who had just saved his life. He was average height, not tall, not short. He had the build of someone who needed to be strong. Not like a weightlifter but someone who needed to use decisive force when necessary. He looked to be in his late thirties. Dark hair peaked out from under his blue and red cap. The front of the cap had a logo depicting a royal crest with a knight's head. The logo read Club Deportivo Chivas USA. The three-day growth on his face gave him the look of an actor in a movie rather than someone who was looking to pick tomatoes. His jeans were covered with dirt and his plaid, long-sleeved shirt was stuck to his body with sweat.

"You speak English pretty well." Drew said, hoping for an explanation.

"My grade school and *preparatoria* were taught by American Holy Cross nuns. We were taught English every day," Gerardo said with a laugh. "Sister Patricia once told me that I was her best student and one day my English would be an important part of my life."

"Out here in the middle of nowhere," Chino said, "it looks like it is pretty damned valuable to us."

"Anyways, I owe my English-speaking skills to the Catholic Church and ESPN Sports Center."

Drew laughed for the first time in what seemed like months to him.

"*Órale, amigos,*" Gerardo said as he brushed clumps of dirt from the front of his jeans, "now that we are all in the same mess, any other questions?"

The four men were silent. Gerardo turned and started walking back to the truck.

"I've got just one question for you," Chance called out from behind.

Gerardo stopped and turned back.

"Who the fuck are you?"

Gerardo thought about it for a few seconds.

"I'm a guy who is either going to live or die with you over the next few hours."

THIRTY-TWO

The GPS locator box was a civilian grade device, but Drew could see that the basic functions were the same. It was a hard-green steel case that opened to display a satellite map and ping mark. As the truck was moving away from the trailer Drew could see the ping remain still.

Chino drove the pickup truck that belonged to the traffickers with Drew in the front passenger seat and Chance and Gerardo in the back.

"How far do we need to go?" Drew asked Gerardo.

"Far enough so that they won't be able to see any dust rising from our vehicle."

Drew looked behind him and then ducked his head low to see the road ahead of him.

"From what it looks like," Drew said as he kept looking back to front, "there is a curve up ahead and the start of some foothills. We can pull into some brush and wait for the GPS to show movement."

Chino continued down the road for another few miles and then saw a power line service road off to the right. He pulled the truck off and followed the service road a half mile. The sky was clear, and the multitude of stars stood out against the night. He backed the truck into some mesquite trees, the branches scraping the top of the truck cab.

There was no mistaking the smell of sweat and blood in the cab of the truck. They sat silent for a couple of minutes before Drew pulled out his firearm to pop the clip.

"Well, Gerardo," he said checking the rounds again, "why the fuck are you really here?"

"I was crossing with the same group that hid the children in the trailer. It started out pretty normal," Gerardo said while looking behind him down the road and then turning toward Drew, "but once I happened to see the children, it turned strange."

"How so?" Chino asked.

"They kept them hidden as much as possible and . . ." he said and paused. "It was really strange the way they were tied together, two by two, like prisoners in a chain gang."

"I take it that none of the rest of you were tied up," Drew said.

"That's right, and it bothered me all night. I knew I should let it alone, but I just couldn't. Each boy was paired with a girl, all the same age, drugged and bound. I kept trying to figure it out."

"Did you ever reach a conclusion?" Drew asked.

"Those poor little kids, six boys and six girls—I knew there was only one reason for them being here."

Drew and Chino said nothing.

"They separated us and packed the children away in the compartment of the trailer," he said as he remembered the scene, "and they put us in a truck."

"Why didn't they deliver you to your destination?" Drew asked.

"That's the thing. Something happened, and they left us stranded in a false compartment in a truck in the middle of the desert."

"Sounds pretty fucked up," Chino said.

"You are right about that, *amigo*. They left us in there to die."

"So why the fuck are you still out here?" Drew asked.

"Well, it's not like I was out here looking for you," Gerardo said with a laugh. "I was hiding in the hills waiting for the night to come to hike my way out when I saw the truck and trailer and then those *pendejos* pulling up in their truck. I knew it was the same truck and trailer that they loaded the children into so I got to a place where I could observe what was going to happen."

"What did it look like from up there in the hills?" Chino asked.

"Like they were getting ready to put a bullet in each one of your heads."

"Well," Drew said, "thanks again for saving our asses. I just hope that you didn't make a mistake in helping us."

"Oh, there's no doubt I made a mistake, a big mistake. I made the mistake of caring about what was going to happen to those kids."

Silence enveloped them for a minute or so.

"What's your background?" Chino finally said. "You police or military?"

"Actually both," Gerardo said as he removed his hat to brush back his sweat-dampened hair. "But for the last ten years, I was with the Federal Police and assigned to assist the Culiacan Police in drug enforcement."

Gerardo paused to consider that last statement and gave a rueful laugh.

"Why did you leave the police?" Drew asked.

"*Tu sabes.* Mexico is what it is, you need to play on both sides to survive. I got tired of playing."

"What the fuck is that supposed to mean?" Chance said.

"It means there's nothing good back home. The cartels run everything. They kill their competitors. They kill the police. They kill their customers. Their competitors kill them." Gerardo paused to think about his statement.

"I got sick and tired of waiting to be the next one to die."

"You worked for the cartels while you were a cop?" Drew asked.

"Not so much worked for them, I was available to them," Gerardo said, emphasizing the word available. "Whenever information was needed, or someone needed to be found."

"What happened when someone was needed to be found?" Chino asked.

"*Pues*," Gerardo slouched and brought the brim of his hat down over his eyes, "*tu sabes*, they ended up face down in the dirt. The same place all of you were going."

"Why the fuck should we trust you then?" Chance asked looking nervously at Gerardo.

Gerardo stayed reclined against the seat with the hat down.

"You shouldn't, but seeing as I killed one of their men and robbed them of the thrill of another desert execution," Gerardo sat erect and pushed the brim of his hat up to look at Chance, "I'm just as dead as you are unless we can end this."

"And how does this end?" Chino asked, although he knew the answer.

"It ends when we cut off the head of the snake."

The others looked at Gerardo in silence.

"Look," Gerardo took on a grave tone, "they will not stop. They will hunt you until they find you. They will hurt your friends and family to get to you. The next Mexican you see in a 7-Eleven, the gas station or Walmart might be the one that puts a bullet in your head. Our only chance is to go to them and put an end to this. If we are to have any hope of being alive in the near future, it's the only way."

Drew sat in contemplation of Gerardo's words. Thoughts raced through his mind. His wife. His children.

"What makes you think that they have not gotten word back to Mexico yet?" Drew asked.

"Pride," Gerardo replied. "Caritas is young and does not want to be seen as weak or incompetent. He will keep silent about this until after he catches us and deals with the problem. The story of how he dealt with the situation is better than how he fucked up."

"So, our game plan is to find them—" Chino said.

"And kill them all," Drew said.

"Even that might not be enough," Gerardo said. "Caritas has deep family ties to Sinaloa cartels. If word gets back to them about our involvement, then we might as well have a big red target painted on our backs. If we can eliminate all of them, maybe we can eliminate the possibility that we can be identified."

"That's a lot of maybes in your plan," Chino said.

"Sometimes maybe is the best you can hope for," Gerardo replied in a somber tone.

THIRTY-THREE

Minutes passed without words. Drew found it hugely frustrating to sit without a phone to call his wife and warn her. Then again, what would he say? Stay away from the house because the traffickers he was working for were coming to kill her and the boys? Could they go to the police? And tell them exactly what?

The sky was dark and clear, and the wind was still blowing warm from the east.

"They're on the move!" Chino shouted.

The exclamation brought Drew out of his depressing daydream.

"Go! Go!" Chance yelled.

"No," Gerardo calmly said, "we have the locator. We can't let them see the headlights."

"Let's give them a couple of miles," Drew said. "I think they probably won't be traveling on any highways or main roads."

"What do you expect we're going to find?" Drew asked Gerardo.

"A ranch house. Surrounded by a fence. There will probably be a large barn or storage shed."

"Secluded," Chino added.

"*Sí*, with anywhere between ten to fifteen men guarding it."

"Can I assume they're not professionals?" Drew asked.

"Professional enough to put a bullet in you."

"How about firepower?" Drew asked.

"Handguns, a rifle or two, most likely an AK or Uzi," Gerardo said, then paused. "They like those submachine guns, harder to miss targets when you are firing hundreds of rounds per minute."

Drew withheld the need to give his own opinion because, as Gerardo said, they were professional or gangster enough to put a bullet in each of them.

"We clearly need to take enough of them as silently as possible before we make any type of move," Drew said as he wiped sweat off his forehead with the back of his hand.

Gerardo let out a loud breath.

"*Mira,*" he said, "I don't know you, where you are from, or what your history is with violence, but I don't want to go in there with someone that is going to get me killed. If I wanted that I would take my chances out on the streets."

Drew started to say something, but Gerardo kept talking.

"About two years ago I got a call from one of the *narco* captains about someone they were looking for. The man skimmed $14,000 from his delivery to pay for an air conditioner for his wife who had been treated for cancer. Chemotherapy. Summer in Los Mochis is deadly hot. It can get up to one hundred and twenty degrees for days. Thing is," Gerardo said as he looked around, "had he just asked for the money, they probably would have given it to him. Instead, he stole small amounts not thinking they would find out."

Gerardo shook his head in disbelief.

"You see, $14,000 is nothing to them. I've seen them burn more than that in a backyard grill to make *carne asada.*"

Chino, Drew, and Chance hung on every word.

"*Pues*, they found out and caught up with him while he was on the run in Obregon. I know because I was there. He did the usual

132

begging for his life, which he knew was pointless. Then he started begging for the life of his wife and family."

"What were you doing there?" Chance asked.

"Does it matter?" Gerardo replied in a somber tone.

"They took him back to his neighborhood in Los Mochis, so that everyone could see that he was back. Cicatriz, *el jefe*, made sure that they brought the man's wife and ten-year-old son to watch. The man continued to beg, even after they peeled off one of his ears with a straight blade and made his son hold it between his teeth. The next ear was for his wife. They let him beg and cry for a full twenty minutes before they opened his throat to let him bleed out on in front of his family."

Gerardo paused a moment at the memory.

"To this day, I have never seen so much blood. I mean that." He looked at each of them. "I have never seen so much blood flowing from one human being in my life." He paused again, "The thing is, nobody cared the least bit. When we walked out of the house, the neighbors went about their business, and Cicatriz told the four men he was with that he knew of a really good family taco restaurant around the corner."

"You went to eat tacos?" Chino asked.

"I went behind the house to throw up. Look, I'm not proud of being there, but at the time, I had already been dragged in. No choice. I could continue my association with them or end up exactly like that guy. Dead."

Gerardo paused again to collect himself. This was the first time he had ever told the story to anyone.

"I decided that I was out that day, I had to get out. I could not be part of something like that. That's why I'm here now. But seeing the children and knowing what was going to happen to them and what was about to happen to you," Gerardo said while running a hand down the sides of his unshaven face and looking for the words, "I had to do something to stop it, to at least put an end to this little pocket of evil. No one was going to die in the dirt if I could help it, and these kids were not going to become some rich *pendejo's* plaything. Maybe that would atone just a little bit for what I let happen. I made that decision hiding up in the hills."

"Well," Chino said, "thanks for making that decision when we were about to get wasted."

"I tell you all this not because I want you to believe that I'm some sort of savior or good man," Gerardo's voice was parched, and he lowered it. "I most definitely am not a good man. I tell you this because these men are not like anyone that you have ever dealt with before. They will not stop."

"Well, it looks like our only chance is to be ready for them," Drew said.

"I can tell two of you were in the military, and that's good. But this is not war. There is no higher purpose, no great cause. These people want to kill us for cold reasons, respect, and vengeance. We need to kill them to survive. This is an old movie, and I've seen the way it usually ends."

"I understand. I don't want my family hurt."

"This is not about being hurt," Gerardo said, "it's about being dead."

"I'm in," Chino said. "Drew and I have been through some shit, it's not anything we haven't seen before."

"How about you, Gordito?" Gerardo said with a flick of his eyes at Chance.

Chance was silent for a moment.

"I don't want to live the rest of my life waiting for some stray Mexican to pop a cap in me. I'm in. Whatever it takes."

Drew looked over at Chance.

"Killing people is not any kind of easy," Drew said. "And these people aren't going to be disarmed."

"The way I see it," Chance said, then paused to consider his words, "is these guys gave up the right to be considered normal people when they decided to become involved with this shit. They have twelve kids that they know are going to be peddled off like pieces of meat. Fuck those guys."

"You took that beating pretty well back there," Gerardo said. "What's make you so tough?"

"I've been having the shit beat out of me all my life." Chance spit blood onto the ground. "My old man beat the shit out of my mom and then, when he was tired of that, he took it out on me. I took it for my mom. You've all heard this kind of story. I didn't have any older brothers or anyone for help. I didn't want the police to come and leave her with no income and an angry, fucked-up husband waiting to get out and kill her."

Chance paused to spit again.

"One day, I had enough of his bullshit. I must have been thirteen or fourteen. He started in on my mom and he was bashing her skull with his closed fist so hard I could hear it from the other room. I grabbed a baseball bat from the baseball team I was kicked off because my dad was a hostile drunk at the games."

He wiped a trickle of blood making its way down his forehead and into his eyes, but the bleeding had mostly stopped.

"Anyways, I came up from behind him as he was about to hit her again and cracked that asshole in the head."

All three men listened without moving as Chance continued. Drew looked at Chino and guessed the outcome.

"Well, according to the medical examiner," Chance said, "it was a one-off, lucky shot. Crushed the brain stem, and it was lights out for the piece of shit."

Chino stared open-mouthed.

"The fucked-up thing was that my mom wouldn't back me up. Said that she had the injuries from the day before after a fall. After some bullshit court case, I ended up in CYA for assault with a deadly weapon."

"I guess it's a good thing it wasn't murder," Chino said.

Chance was not amused. Memories of the California Youth Authority hadn't faded.

"CYA is basically juvie prison. For a white boy like me, it was hell. I knew nobody, had no neighborhood or gang ties. No protection. It was constant fighting, beatings by other inmates and staff. The long and short of it was that I took a lot more than I gave out."

Chance somehow found value in the experience and laughed.

"I guess you can say I developed a very high pain threshold from getting the shit kicked out of me."

He paused for a moment, his shoulder and face bearing witness to his resolve.

"But don't get me wrong, I can throw down like a motherfucker if I have to. I say we need wipe these bastards out."

Drew jumped in. "Listen to me—"

"No, dude, these guys will kill or torture for fun or on command and, more fucked up, they are trafficking these kids to be sold off to sick fucks. No, fuck them, whatever it takes to end this, I'm in."

"What it will take," Gerardo said, "is that every single one of them has to be dead."

Drew knew he was right, but he also knew there was a gigantic difference between firing at someone shooting at you in a foreign country and killing people in your own backyard.

"That means no wounded left behind. No charity cases. No witnesses," Gerardo delivered the words slowly and calmly.

Conversation ceased for a few minutes, then Drew turned to Chino.

"Let's roll."

"Copy that."

THIRTY-FOUR

Tracking the trailer with the GPS was simple. The box displayed a satellite image and map, and the green locator dot moved in small increments down demarcated roads and dotted lanes. They could tell when the trailer left the paved roads because the dot moved off the lined street routes. The dot came to a resting point and stayed stationary for over five minutes before Drew decided it was time to move toward it.

"From the satellite, it looks like they are about nine miles outside of Jacumba, off Old Highway 80," Drew said as he scanned the GPS.

"There's nothing out there," Chance said.

Gerardo said, "Sounds like the type of place that you want to be if you are a smuggler."

Drew continued to view the GPS.

"There are some foothills in the area, the place may even be backed against a canyon."

Chino drove along a barely visible dirt road. They left the roadway about five minutes ago and stayed under ten miles an hour to avoid kicking up too much dust.

He said, "We need to ditch these headlights soon. It's so dark out here they look like spotlights."

Drew said while focused on the GPS map, "Looks like we're about one klick out. We need to find a place to stash the truck and hump it in."

Chance tapped Chino on the shoulder. "Over on the right looks like a good spot."

The road continued straight until a sharp turnoff led behind a stand of trees. Chino cut the lights and pulled the truck off the road and drove slowly behind the trees. He found a place that was not visible from the road and backed in.

"Just in case we need to push the eject button in a hurry," Chino said.

All four got out of the pickup without saying a word. Drew looked around. From the ambient light, he could make out the terrain. Low-lying hills peppered with stumpy mesquite trees and desert chaparral. A few lone cactuses thrown in for good measure.

The three men looked to Drew for instruction.

"Let's give this truck the once over and see if there is anything we can use."

Drew entered the passenger side and looked in the glove case. A small folding tactical knife with a sharp three-inch blade was buried beneath crumpled receipts and two empty plastic water bottles. He also found a lighter and a ten-inch Maglite. Drew covered the lens, thumbed the switch, and saw that it worked. He looked underneath the seats and behind the back bench seat. No additional weapons.

Chino popped his head in the driver's side.

"What you thinking, Drew?"

Drew opened the knife and began to cut away the seatbelts. He pulled five long straps out and split each one down the middle lengthwise with the knife.

"Gonna need to make a ghillie."

Chino nodded in agreement.

"What the fuck is a ghillie?" Chance asked.

Chino turned to explain.

"A ghillie suit is a sniper's armor," he said as a grating sound arose from Drew's work with the knife. "The suit is covered with natural vegetation, shrubs, plant—"

"The idea," Drew said, "is to camouflage your body on the ground. You need to eliminate your outline in the scenery."

"The sniper crawls very slowly to a point of advantage for the kill shot," Chino finished.

"The human eye is very attuned to movement," Drew said. "What you want to do is limit the amount of sudden movement and also have no sharp lines to attract attention or comparison."

"Were you in the special forces?" Gerardo asked.

"No. Just a kick-ass devil dog Marine Corps sniper."

"Sounds good enough for me," Gerardo considered his own clothing after hearing what Drew had to say.

"With these straps," Drew said, holding up the long ribbons of seat belt webbing, "I'll be able to attach the scenery and background that I need. I can get within a few feet of these motherfuckers if I have to, but for now I just need to get close enough to figure out our play."

"Hey, Drew," Chance said, "you think we can siphon off some gas with one of the motor hoses to fill those water bottles?"

"Nice idea, Gordo," Gerardo said, reaching in to pull the latch on the hood. "One never knows when he will have to send someone to hell."

"I'm kinda of sick of you calling me that, homey."

"I don't know," Drew said, "it's kind of growing on me."

"Me too," said Chino.

THIRTY-FIVE

They made their way up a ridgeline that ran northwest. Gerardo led the way with Drew behind. Chance and Chino brought up the rear as they climbed single file up a narrow game trail. The desert temperature was starting to drop into the mid-fifties, but all the men were sweating from the physical activity and nervous fear. The night sky was ink black, and Gerardo had to place each step carefully to navigate the trail. Drew and the others duplicated the man in front's step as if negotiating a minefield. They moved slowly; no one said a word.

Gerardo could see the top of the ridge a few yards ahead of him. He could also see the faint glow of lights beyond. He stopped and held his hand up for the others to stop.

"*Alto*," Gerardo whispered. "Looks like we are here."

Drew scurried to the top of the ridge on all fours, and the others crawled behind him. The ground was thick, coarse sand mixed with rocks. Sharp, hard edges jutted out and caused biting pain as they dragged themselves across the dirt. Once at the top, they could see the layout below them. The ranch sat at the bottom of a small canyon. Two structures, one large two-story house and what looked to be a barn. They couldn't make out the color in the dark. The house had the run-down look of years without paint. The roofing was peeling off near the peak. It appeared to have multiple rooms. No lights on in the second story, but the bottom floor probably had a large living area. The curtains were drawn, but people could be seen moving around. There were three pickup trucks and a Cadillac Escalade, the same one Caritas was in when they met him. Some fifty yards away was a barnlike structure made of corrugated steel. One of its corners abutted the hillside. The lights were off. A western-style split-rail fence surrounding the house. The fence perimeter stood about fifty yards from the house. The fence posts were about six feet apart, the cross pieces started about two feet from the ground. Drew could see he would have no problem crawling under the fence. The fencing converged at an iron gate at the base of a fifty-foot-long dirt driveway. The gate was open.

Gerardo gestured with his hand, pointing at the structure. "The trailer is behind the barn." He could see the back end of the trailer and the racing stripe.

"Most likely the kids are in there," said Chino, lifting his head for a better view.

"Can you tell how many guys are down there?" Chance asked.

"My guess," Gerardo said, "three trucks, the Escalade, ten to twelve men. Expect all of them to be armed. Maybe four with training, the others just cowboys with guns."

"Fuck," Chance winced in pain, "fucking cactus!"

He had rolled onto a small cactus coming up through the dirt and now had twenty or thirty small spines implanted in his right thigh.

"Should have rethought those shorts," Drew said.

Gerardo said, "Quit moving around. You're kicking up a dust cloud."

"Fuck! Fuck! Fuck!" Chance said in a barely suppressed whisper.

"Okay," Drew said, "I will slide down the hill and make my way over to the barn. I've got the Maglite. I will signal with one flash when I get there. The best thing to do is for one of us, looks like me in this case, to get to the top of the barn. From that position, I can fire on them in multiple directions. Also looks high enough to give me cover while firing. It might be that I find a better spot when I get down there."

Drew surveyed the area for a few seconds.

"Chino. Gerardo. If you get close enough to take anyone of these guys out without a discharging your weapon, make the move. Otherwise, just look for the signal or when I start firing. If I can take out a few of them along the way, all the better. Even better if one of them happens to have a rifle."

"Better yet with a scope, right Drew?" Chino said.

"We can always hope."

Drew surveyed the ranch site and canyon for a few more moments.

"It's going to take me about twenty minutes to make my way over there. Chance, you stay here. Gerardo, you flank right. Chino, you go left. I am going to wait ten full minutes before I do anything."

"What exactly are you going to do?" asked Gerardo.

"Haven't figured that out yet."

"Nice plan," Chance said, sounding nervous.

"All you need to know is that after the first shot," Drew looked to Gerardo and then to Chino, "you move in. Shoot anything that moves."

"Remember, anyone of them gets out," Gerardo paused and looked at all three, "we and our families are dead."

Drew thought long and hard about all of them making the leap to killing. This was not self-defense. They were stalking these men.

They were using the element of surprise to kill as many as they could. He did the same in Iraq and Afghanistan, but this was different. He accepted death in war, at least he could sleep with the deaths he caused. These deaths would be pre-emptive and for self-preservation. Regardless of the reason, he thought, death was final and would come for many, maybe even him, very soon.

THIRTY-SIX

Gerardo watched intently as Drew assembled his ghillie suit. Drew wrapped two of the bands across his back, one on the back of each thigh and calf. Chino helped him find brush and other dry grasses to start attaching to the bands across his backside. Drew found two good sized tumbleweeds and attached them to a brace of mesquite branches. He fashioned a handle by bending two branches in an arc and securing them into to the brace.

"I can use these as cover and push them in front of me as I crawl forward."

Chino moved forward to adjust one of the straps across Drew's chest. He flattened the dark blue shirt with the yellow lightning bolt with his hand. "It's a good thing that Charger T isn't one of those powder blues."

Drew brushed his palm down the front of his dark blue T-shirt. He felt particularly guilty because Katie had just bought the shirt for him. Even now he was worried about how he might upset her.

"How do you move with all that stuff on?" Chance asked.

"You move as slowly as possible," Drew answered. The ghillie acts to blur my outline in case any of these *narco* cowboys thinks they saw something move in the distance."

"How close can you get to them?" Gerardo asked.

"If this were my service ghillie," Drew said as he was standing and adjusting the brush across his shoulders, "I could punch them in the balls."

"But given the fact you have pieced this together like a Mexican *llantaria* shop—" Gerardo started to say.

"Probably fifty feet," Drew finished.

Chance handed Drew one of the water bottles filled with gasoline.

"Still don't know what we are going to do with these," Chance said, "but I figure you should take one with you. It might come in handy."

"Anyone have a lighter or matches?" Drew asked.

Gerardo reached into his front pocket and tossed him a Zippo lighter.

"Just so that we're clear," Drew said while looking around at all of them, "unless you've got a clean move on one of these guys without firing a weapon, nobody makes a move until I signal, or you hear any gunfire. Copy?"

"Copy that," Chino said.

"Got it," Chance said while still trying to pull cactus spines out of his thigh.

"*Sí, señor*," Gerardo said with a nod.

"Ammo check," Drew said, pulling out his weapon.

They all rechecked their clips for a recount and snapped them back in, the metallic sounds giving some measure of security to them.

"So," Drew said while readjusting the shrubs attached to the lashing around his arms and legs, "make sure everyone stays high on the ridge until I signal. If I give a signal, that means that I'm in position, and you should start making your way down."

"I'm figuring it will take us five to seven minutes, slow moving, to get down the canyon floor," Chino said.

"Like I said, we need to take out anyone we can hand-to-hand, before any shots get fired," Drew said while looking at Chance. "Chino is trained to do this, and Gerardo, I don't know, something tells me has done something like this before."

Gerardo nodded.

"So, Chance, I need you to bat clean up."

Chance started to say something, but Drew kept talking. "Look, it's one thing to talk about, and a whole other to do it in real life. I don't doubt that you could perform, but I just don't want to take the gamble."

"You don't need to worry about me—"

"What he is saying is that it is one thing to kill someone when you are angry or in self-defense," Gerardo said as he reached into his pocket to pull out the folding knife. "It is most definitely another thing to take someone's life when they are not . . ." he opened the blade on the knife and thrust it forward in the air, ". . . expecting it."

"Look, Chance," Drew continued, "we are all in this together. To get out of this, we are going to have to do some pretty drastic shit. But these cowboys knew what they were signing up for when they joined up with this gang."

"They are by no means," Gerardo almost whispered, "innocent."

"What I need to know," Drew said and approached Chance to put his hand on his shoulder, "is can we count on you to listen to me and do what you need to do?"

Chance adjusted his bloody shirt mostly for something to do with his hands. His leg still stung from the cactus spines, his face and head were covered with dried, caked, and dirty blood.

"Are you good to go?" Chino said, deliberate with each word.

"You can count on me. Just tell me what I need to do."

"First thing you need to know is that you won't hit shit with that pistol unless you are close. You have no training, and the weapon is made primarily to defend in close quarters," Drew said and reached out with his palm up.

Chance handed him the weapon, butt first. Drew held the gun out with arms extended.

"Two hands," Drew said, his right hand on the pistol grip and his left hand cupping the base of his right hand. "None of this TV gangster one-handed shit."

Chance nodded, sensing the seriousness of the situation.

"Center mass. Aim for the largest part of the body. At least two shots from that position," Drew said and watched Chance's eyes to gauge whether he was grasping his instructions.

"And for fuck's sake, don't stand around to watch the results of the firing. Keep moving, don't make yourself a target."

"*Mira,* Gordo," Gerardo said, "I can tell you for a fact that except for maybe one or two of them, none of these *pendejos* is going to be very accurate from a distance. So keep moving. Keep low."

"You copy all that, Chance?" Chino asked.

"Got it," he said but sounded nervous. "Shoot center mass, keep low, keep moving."

The other three nodded in silent approval. Drew turned to make his way back up the ridge for another look at the scene in the canyon when he stopped and turned back to Chance.

"One more thing," he said. "What the fuck type of nickname is Chance?"

No response.

"What's your real name?"

Chance hesitated before he replied.

"My name is Chester."

Drew half smiled.

"Now I know I like Gordo better."

Chino and Gerardo stifled their amusement.

"Feeling better with Gordo at my side than some dude named Chance," Drew said.

Chance smiled and gave it time to sink in.

"*Pues, ándale,*" Gerardo said, "Gordo it is. Hopefully, we will be able to call you that tomorrow."

THIRTY-SEVEN

Drew steadied himself before he set out over the ridge, the same routine he used on missions. Deep clearing breath. One one thousand. Two one thousand. Three one thousand. Clear the machine. Another deep breath. One one thousand. Two one thousand. Three one thousand. Focus on the heart rate. Bring the vein-bulging, heart-racing rush of adrenaline and fear down to a manageable level. With each mind-cleansing breath, Drew focused on his heart rate. A consciousness of his internal organ that he tried to control. Cool. Calm. Steady the mind for the task ahead. On missions, Drew would repeat to himself a mantra he developed to aid his concentration. I am a Weapon. I am the Dark. I am the Silence. I am Death.

Drew's training taught him how to move, how to kill. His own experience taught him how to meld the training with the movements of his own body. He knew he naturally favored his right shoulder, which meant his right side was higher than the other while crawling on his belly. He knew his left knee dragged for a few inches farther than his right. He knew that from the prone position, he could get to his feet and cover forty yards, with a rifle in hand, in 5.6 seconds. He knew his internal body temperature ran at 98.9 degrees and, although he had no medical proof, he believed he could control the amount of fog his breath made in the cold. For that reason, he always held his breath and breathed into the ground. All these factors were unique to his body and his mindset. Drew believed that understanding these factors and working with them could mean the difference between life and death.

Drew found himself thinking of these things as he made his way down the hill. Slow and deliberate. No movement was wasted. The brush attached to his backside blended in with the vegetation along the trail. He felt like he was in a protective cocoon. The familiar feeling of invisibility began to surround him, and he gained confidence in his movements. Inching along, ground at eye level, Drew could not believe how much he missed the danger. How much he missed melting into the scenery. He sighted the barn, which looked like it was built within inches of the hillside. He could see two men stationed outside the main house. Drew was not close enough to make out any description or whether they were armed. He assumed they were. He could also see two men, one standing next to a pickup and the other sitting on the open bed, tailgate down. The truck was just to the right of the barn. The trailer that held the children was parked to the left of the truck.

The night was cool, he estimated maybe 55 degrees. Drew could see his breath as he exhaled to the side. He slowed down the release of his breath and exhaled low into the dirt. As the evening progressed, a quarter moon had risen over the hills and gave off just enough illumination to let him make sense of the scene below him. No ambient sound. Save for a lone coyote howl in the distance, it was silent. Drew concentrated on each movement. Right shoulder forward, push the screen two or three feet. Right knee up across the dirt. He could hear the grinding of the coarse dirt. Left shoulder forward. Drew kept focused on his movements. With each movement, he considered how it would look to anyone scanning the hillside. He knew he had the advantage that the men below him were not professional soldiers, nor were they in active combat or at war. Wartime and constant fear of death made a man uniquely aware of his environment. Any noise or light disturbance would attract your eyes and ears, senses awakened, gun at the ready. The most these guys were looking for was maybe a Border Patrol helicopter or the lights of a moving vehicle that they would be able to see about a mile away.

From up on the ridge and to the left, Gerardo watched Drew move with deliberation and calculation. He was impressed with Drew's patience and economy of movement. When Drew was forty to fifty yards away, Gerardo could barely find him on the hillside even though he knew where to look.

Chino and Chance also watched.

"I was with Drew on a mission in Kandahar," Chino whispered to Gerardo, "and the only way to get a clean shot was to scurry down a ravine and then into a dry gully. Looked to be about two hundred yards to travel. Watched him move for almost an hour."

Gerardo and Chance kept their eyes on Drew as Chino spoke.

"The target looked to be about two hundred feet away when I see this light coming toward Drew's position."

"You radio him to get the fuck out of there?" Chance asked.

"No, I just told him that he had a hostile heading his way."

Gerardo raised himself on his forearms for a better view. Drew looked about three-quarters of the way down the hillside.

"Anyways," Chino continued, "Drew can't move because he will get seen, so he just maintains his position. Lying in the dirt. In the dark. In his ghillie."

Chino paused for a moment.

"All of a sudden, haji comes and stops on the lip of the gully within about five feet of Drew."

"Holy shit," Chance whispered.

"The light turns out to be this dude's phone," Chino said and laughed at the memory. "Then the fucking crazy thing is that this motherfucking Taliban, this Allah-loving terrorist drops his baggy ass rag pants, pulls his dick out and starts jacking off to something on his phone!"

"What was he looking at?" Chance asked.

"How the fuck should I know?" Chino gave Chance a look of disbelief. "Whatever it was, Asian porn or a guy fucking a camel, he was out there to beat his meat."

"What was your friend doing?" Gerardo asked.

"Lying perfectly still, face down, in his ghillie, in the shit dirt, in a fucking dry creek bed, in fuck-this-shit Afghanistan." Chino stopped to catch his breath.

"Then what?" Chance asked as if he did not know what the answer was going to be.

"What do you mean, then what?" Chino said as he looked at Chance with a smirk.

"Well, I mean . . . er," Chance started to say.

"He grabbed that haji by the ankle, yanked him to the ground and drove his knife into his throat, OJ style. Not a sound, not a cloud of dust. Over in one second. One-minute dude is yanking it to dreams of one thousand virgins, the next he's watching a bush drive a knife down his neck—probably with his dick still in his hand."

Gerardo let out a short, nasal laugh, and Chance was silent, maybe trying to picture the scene.

"You want to know what it looked like from where I was watching?" Chino asked.

Gerardo and Chance exchanged glances and waited for the response.

"It looked like the dirt rose up and swallowed him."

A palpable stillness surrounded them for a few moments as they all tried to spot the moving bush.

"It appears we have the right man for the job," Gerardo said. "He is almost down; we should start to get into position."

"Copy that," Chino replied.

"*Oye, Gordo,* make sure your weapon is on safety while you are crawling around. We don't want that thing to go off."

"I'm not that stupid." Chance reached down his waistband to finger the safety on the Sig. It was off. He engaged it.

"Of course, when you get down there you disengage that shit," Chino said in a deliberate cadence. "Got it?"

"Don't worry about me. I got it."

"One more thing," Chino said with a direct look at Chance, "the Alamo is the truck and trailer."

"The Alamo?" Chance asked, realization taking the slow route to his face.

"Our rally point, where we fight backs to the wall." Chino looked over the ridge at the barn and trailer.

"One question, though."

Chino and Gerardo looked directly at him.

"Didn't everyone die at the Alamo?"

All three broke into laughter.

"Pretty much," Chino said, reaching to put his hand on Chance's shoulder, "but they took a fuck ton of Mexicans with them."

Chino looked over at Gerardo.

"No offense."

"None taken," Gerardo said with a nod. "It was a glorious defeat."

The night sky had taken on the color of deep blue fading to black. The quarter moon lit the canyon softly. From their vantage point, at least six armed men were visible. They weren't outside to offer a friendly welcome.

"If they see you, they won't fire warning shots," Gerardo said to Chance and Chino.

"They'll be shooting to kill," Chino added.

"Any military advice?" Chance asked Chino.

"Yeah," he said as he rechecked his firearm. "Don't get shot in the back."

Chance gave him a puzzled look.

"Once the shooting starts, stay low, move fast, move forward," Gerardo said.

"Copy that."

The three men looked at each other for a moment when Chance laughed a bit.

"What could be so funny right now?" Chino asked.

"I've been waiting my whole life to say that."

"*Ándale, pues,*" Gerardo said as he turned to make his way to the flank of the ridge. "The attack of El Gordo begins."

"You know," Chance said to Chino, "it's kind of growing on me."

"What is?"

"Gordo."

"Well," Chino said in an exaggerated Western twang while he made sure his weapon was secure in his waistband, "Gordo, let's go fuck some shit up and get those kids."

"Copy that."

THIRTY-EIGHT

Drew was within twenty-five yards of two men standing guard near the barn. He was not moving, frozen solid to the ground behind the shrub screen he pushed. He found himself in an advantageous position, in a dry, narrow creek where the grasses and mesquite had grown tall and wild on the sides. From this position, he could hear them speak.

Fuck! Can't understand a word. Just one more reason in a thousand why I should have learned Spanish in this part of the country where half the population speaks it.

Drew continued his personal protocol. He steadied his breathing. Even as close as he was, his heart rate was steady and slow. From his concealment, Drew felt that his awareness of sound, time, and movement was enhanced. The carnal feeling of predatory behavior was intoxicating. Drew knew that, for the moment, he wielded enormous power. He knew this was because the enemy did not know he was there. I am a Weapon. I am the Dark. I am the Silence. I am Death.

The two men were standing next to the bed of the pickup, which was now unhitched from the trailer. Drew saw they were older, maybe forty, and overweight. One had his back to Drew while the other was facing in Drew's direction. A Tec-9 hung from a strap around the right shoulder of the man who faced Drew. The other had a handgun shoved into the back of his waistband. Drew had handled a Tec-9 once at a firing range. It belonged to a friend who purchased it at a gun show. The short, powerful looking nine-millimeter with a thirty-round clip look menacing. The reality, Drew found, is that it's not very accurate. It is practically impossible to aim, and it jerked up and viciously to the right when it was being fired. He surmised this cowboy had only test fired this thing while drinking beers in the desert and murdering an unfortunate cactus or two. From the way it was hanging from his shoulder, Drew figured it would take him four to five seconds t to reach around his ample middle, grab the handle, pull the strap off his shoulder, and point it in any general direction. After that, he would only be firing haphazardly. It would be difficult for this amateur to redirect the rounds with any accuracy. As for the other guard, anyone who had a weapon tucked into the back of a waistband at a critical moment was asking to be killed.

Drew scanned the entire site. There was significant movement in the house. He could see bedsheets had been tacked up as curtains. The lights were on, and he could see bodies moving about inside. The barn had a dim light coming from inside. About three or four men were standing around the entrance to the main house. He needed to be in a position to take out these two by the pickup before any firing started. Without any outside lights, the night provided decent cover. He began to make his way around the perimeter and kept himself squarely in the shadows.

About twenty yards into his torturously slow crawl he looked back at the ridge where the others were supposed to be waiting. From his position, he could see no movement, no outlines. Good. He wasn't worried about Chino giving up his position. The dirty cop turned child protector could hold his own and was smart enough to lay still. Chance, on the other hand, although he proved he could take a beating, was still a doughy kid trying not to act like he was shitting in his pants. The way he wasted Sunglasses was surprising, but most people are capable of violence when they are in fight-or-flight mode.

This was different. This was calculated, lying in wait. This required coolness and calm in the face of extreme violence. Taking a life was no easy thing. Even in war, there was always that millisecond of regret. He had been trained to ignore it, but it was always there. Drew worried about the possibility Chance would fail when the time came. At this point, worry is all it could be. Drew had no choice but to continue and hope that everyone performed. The life of their families was on the line as well as those of the children who were drugged and likely in the barn.

He made his way to a point about thirty-five yards to the right of the men and about half that distance to the back of the barn. The back side of the barn faced the canyon wall and would provide the best cover for his next move. He scrabbled a few more feet to the right to position himself for the move to the barn. As he steadied himself, Drew noticed that his heart and respiration rates were rising. Like he had on unfamiliar lands in Middle Eastern countries, Drew made a conscious effort to slow his system down. Now, here is his own backyard, his home, he went into attack mode. He closed his eyes. Deep, slow breath. Clear the mind. With his eyes closed, as he had on so many occasions, Drew knew that when they opened again it would be to scan and measure the distance to the target. The target was the man he was going to kill. Deep, slow breath. I am a Weapon. I am the Dark. I am the Silence. I am Death.

THIRTY-NINE

Gerardo could barely make out the outline of Drew's body as he moved across the canyon floor. The movement he saw from afar looked no different than brush moving in a slight breeze. He was impressed with the soldier's patience and skill. He could see Drew was now within twenty yards of the armed men by the barn. He began his descent into the canyon.

On his stomach, Gerardo began a slow, sliding crawl. He tried as best as he could to mimic Drew's movements. Inches at a time, exhaling into the dirt. From his position, he could make out the outlines of Chino and Chance. They had not begun to move yet, and he could now see that Chance had moved over forty yards or so from where he had been waiting. Gerardo continued his gaze past the area where Chino was lying and noticed the dirt begin to partition. The outlines of the partition could only be seen from a distance. The more he looked at it, the more it began to take on the appearance of a road.

"*Puta madre!*" Gerardo muttered to himself. It really was a road. They hadn't seen it when they arrived.

Chance had moved unwittingly toward the access road, which looked like it passed within ten yards of Chance's position before it snaked its way down the canyon.

"*Baboso Gordo!*" he couldn't help but say it out loud.

There was no way to warn him. Gerardo would be seen if he traversed the top rim of the canyon. In any event, he was already halfway down the side of the canyon. Reversing his track was not an option. All he could do was hope no one came down that road for the next half hour or so.

Chino noticed the same thing. The difference was Chino's training taught him the mission should be aborted. Assaults under cover were supposed to be carried out with precision. The proximity of the road to Chance was a factor that needed to be dealt with, but there was no way of contacting him. While Chino's training screamed at him to turn around and fix the situation or abort, the reality was he could not make it over to Chance without being seen. His only choice was to proceed as planned and hope the road remained clear.

Chance was too busy worrying about not being seen or killed to think about looking behind him as he moved laterally for a better view. Unlike Drew, Chance's heart rate was screaming. He could feel the blood rushing through the vein across his forehead and, in the quiet backcountry, could hear his heart pounding. His breathing began to become more rapid.

Pull it together, man.

He tried to remember the breathing technique that Drew and Chino had talked about. He took a deep breath in but found that holding it in only made him more anxious. He let the breath out and, again, tried to calm himself.

He considered his situation. Lying face down in the course gravely dirt with dried blood caked on his head and face. The throbbing sting of the cactus spines still embedded in his thigh intermittently diverted the pain from the pounding headache. He was in this deep. He was going to kill someone or be killed. The whole thing was supposed to be simple, so safe. They weren't transporting drugs, just aliens—gardeners, maids. This thing had blown up. This was not what he signed up for. It was so . . . what was it these military dudes called it?

FUBAR.

Fuck it. Time to fuck some shit up.

Chance propped himself up on his elbows for a better look when he was distracted by the long shadow his head and torso were making on the dirt ahead of him.

Gerardo, Drew, and Chino saw it at the same time.

The headlights of a vehicle coming up the dirt road, the road that escaped their earlier observations. Chance didn't notice the shift in lighting in the trees and shrubs behind him. What got his attention was the unmistakable whine of an engine. Someone was coming. By the time Chance turned around, he was directly in the headlight beams.

He froze.

FORTY

The noise from the horn of the vehicle pierced the backcountry silence like a fire alarm. Drew could see movement inside the house, and the two men in front of him started moving toward the sound with their weapons in hand.

Fuck. Drew knew at that instant Chance had screwed up. He had to improvise. Men came pouring out of the house. He counted least six men moving quickly to the vehicles. Some got into the pickup and an SUV while four others ran to the front gates. All of their backs were to Drew, so he used the opportunity to get to a position near the house without anyone seeing him. Drew made his way to the back of the house. Now that he was close, he could tell the house was much older than it appeared from the canyon rim. Maroon clapboard made up the siding of the house, which was perched on top of a crawlspace. He walked stealthily along the back of the house until he found a rusty metal screen. Drew pried the screen off with the folding knife and peered inside the crawlspace. He could see nothing but darkness and dirt floor. He entered slowly on his stomach and crawled along the dirt. A few rays of light illuminated the dirt floor from the openings in the old wood plank floor above.

Drew knew the commotion would have everyone's attention at the front gates and in the vehicles. There was nothing he could do about them from here. He assessed the situation from a combat mode. Drew knew he could be more effective in the environment he knew best. The dark. He realized he left the screen in the dirt outside the opening, so he crawled back to the opening to reposition the screen. As he was wedging the screen, he was able to get a clear view of the barn where he figured the children being held. In all the planning and positioning, he had forgotten the main reason they were there. He observed the barn long enough to determine there was no lock on the main door, and there appeared to be a side door with a glass window that was out of any light. Drew slowly slid away from the screen and unlashed the belts that were holding the brush he had been using for cover. Free of the excess, he began to look up for access points to the house.

Chance remained frozen, which is what most people would do. The approaching lights tracked in on him like lasers. The vehicle lights were nearly in front of him before he thought about his weapon. Chance pulled the gun out and pulled the trigger. Nothing. Fuck, he realized, the safety. In the time it took him to realize that the safety was still on, it was too late.

The last thing he remembered was the muted sound of a gun firing. In that nanosecond, he mused that it sounded like a cap gun or a small firecracker. But that was right before fire hot pain exploded in his shoulder. Chance had been on his knees but was now on his back staring straight up into the starry night when the figures of men surrounded him. He was able to make out the butt of the rifle as it was coming down toward him.

"*Ay, Gordito,*" Gerardo said to himself in a whisper, "you fucked up." From his vantage point he watched the event unfold. He knew there was nothing he could do. He also knew they would not kill him on the spot. *Narcos* and *polleros* were always wary that someone might try to muscle in on their businesses. That meant they needed information out of Gordo, and that would require a fair amount of force. No true outlaw would miss an opportunity to torture some *pobre pendejo* before putting a bullet through his head. Gerardo knew Gordo's mistake created his best opportunity to make it to the house.

The element of surprise was gone. Their best hope was that the men would let their guard down a bit while they tortured Chance. He would either cough up information immediately or endure a great amount of pain before they killed him. In any event, it would all be over in a few minutes. One way or another.

As he lay on his back in the dark, it occurred to Gerardo that the mission had now changed from an attack to a rescue. A mission to rescue the children, Chance and themselves.

Fuck! Fuck! Chino was blaming himself for bringing Chance out to do a job for which he was not fit. Chino had been on missions that had gone from clockwork to FUBAR in seconds. He was trained to improvise, adapt, and rely on his brothers. He didn't know Gerardo, but he knew he wasn't stupid. Chino knew Drew like his own shadow. He knew Drew would use the distraction to his advantage and move toward the house. That was the only play.

Chino lined up the house and started his run low and fast down a single-track path. When the path intersected a dry creek bed about thirty yards from the house, he dropped to the ground and began to cover himself with dry mesquite brush. He used his forearms to push about two or three inches of dirt out from under his torso. Chino knew the drill, deep breath in and exhale. Breathe and exhale. Concentrate on his heart rate to bring it down.

Chino did his best to remain motionless and chart out his sprint to the house in his mind. Thirty yards. From a dead drop to the house, four seconds. Four seconds to life and, certainly for someone, death.

FORTY-ONE

The sensation of drowning brought Chance out of his deep dark sleep. His face was dripping water, and he could not breathe. He tried to reach up to his face, but his hands wouldn't move. He realized his hands were tied behind him. His jaw was throbbing with intense pain, and the burning in his right shoulder was only slightly less painful. Although he knew he had two eyes, Chance could only see out of the left one. He heard voices yelling but could not make out the words.

Another rush of water followed by a bracing blow to his jaw. The pain spread like a bolt of lightning through his entire body. He looked around and could make out two figures directly in front of him, but he could also make out the outlines of several others standing behind them.

"*Dónde están los otros?*" one yelled as he brought another blow to the same side of his face.

Chance could not have answered if he wanted. His jaw was swollen to the point that it felt like he did not have enough physical energy to open his mouth.

"*Habla al pinche gringo en inglés!*" one of the voices said with a loud laugh.

"Where are your friends, *pendejo!*" the figure in front of him stuck the cold steel barrel of his handgun directly into the wound in Chances shoulder.

The pain was unbearable, but it brought Chance to a fully conscious state.

"I asked you a question, Gordo," the man said as he twisted the barrel in the bleeding hole.

For an instant, Chance wondered to himself why everyone was so quick to call him Gordo, but the thought vanished with the crack of a gun butt across his face. The blow unleashed a new and even more excruciating wave of pain. Chance could not see. He could not make out any sounds. He felt himself drifting out of consciousness when one of the men grabbed him by the hair to hold him up.

"*Cálmate, Nacho,*" said a calm voice. The group went silent.

The man who spoke moved forward, and the others parted and made way for him.

Chance could see now that this was Caritas.

"You know the score, Gordito," Caritas said in a cold, measured cadence. "We know what you did, and this will not end well for you."

Chance could not respond. There was nothing he could say. He tried to open his mouth but could only mumble slurred words.

Caritas moved in front of Chance, bent down, and put his hands on Chance's thighs. Caritas' face was within two inches of Chance. The overpowering talcum smell of his cologne made Chance want to throw up.

"Tell us where the others are, and we can end all of this," Caritas moved his hand toward the open wound. Chance braced himself for the pain.

"You can live through a good five hours of this . . ." Caritas slammed his fist into the wound.

The blow radiated heat and caused his entire right side to go numb.

"Motherfucker! Motherfucker!" Chance howled while spitting blood.

"*Mira, Gordo,*" Caritas said and stood up straight. "Best you start talking before I let one of my boys start peeling your skin."

Caritas let out a chuckle and looked back to the ten or so men behind who seemed to laugh as a group. Chance straightened up his chair, hands still bound behind his back with what he guessed was duct tape. Fucking Mexicans and duct tape. The thought made him smile.

"What's so fucking funny, Gordo?" Caritas grabbed Chance by the chin and held his face up.

Chance began to move his mouth, but words did not immediately emerge. He managed only a low guttural moan as he tried to move his jaw.

"What the fuck you saying, *puto*?"

"Why . . ." Chance could barely form the words and then had to spit out a wad of blood and mucus.

"Why what?" Caritas tilted his head to one side like a dog trying to make out a command.

"Why the fuck," Chance slowly enunciated. "Why the fuck," he stopped to spit out some more blood. "Why does everyone . . ." he spit out more blood.

"Why what?" Caritas asked.

"Why the fuck," Chance slurred out and panned the room with his good eye, "does everyone call me Gordo?" He laughed and spat again.

The last thing he saw was the trail of spit and blood that hit the floor before he lost consciousness from the blow to the head Caritas delivered with the barrel end of his gun.

Drew watched it all from below. As much as he disliked Chance from the beginning, he admired his toughness in the face of near-certain death. After the last blow, he could hear someone yelling at Chance and saw them slap at this face to try to wake him. Time was running out. From a mission perspective, the time to strike was now. It looked like most of the men were gathered around Chance. Only a few were likely to be outside standing guard, and he would have to rely on Chino and Gerardo to move quickly once the attack began. He thought that a shot from below the floorboards would produce one dead man and plenty of confusion. Naturally, they would head to the windows to see who was firing at them. He would have to deliver another shot that would unmistakably be coming from below them to draw their attention away from the outside and back inside.

There were clear gaps in the floorboards of the old house, but none was big enough for an unobstructed shot. Drew's sniper training had involved the study of bullet trajectory. More specifically the external forces that could alter the trajectory of a bullet. Along with the knowns such as weather, water, and wind, there were unknowns. Things like the angle of the barrel or surfaces the bullet would penetrate at the beginning, middle, or at the end of its journey to the target. From a short distance, barrel against the floorboard opening and the short distance to the piece of shit standing above him, the ricochet from the bullet impacting wood might be a bit easier to anticipate. The trick would be to find a gap that was sufficiently even on both sides and close enough to Chance where he could ensure someone would be standing.

Drew slid slowly on his back, careful not to make any noise, to the area where Chance was tied to the chair. He noticed a ray of light coming down about three feet in front of Chance. He made his way there. From his back to the floorboard was about two and a half feet. The gap looked to be about a quarter inch wide. Drew tried to visualize the trajectory of the bullet as it left the chamber, traveled through the barrel and made contact, first with the wood and then the target. The distance was short, so there was a high probability of striking a target. He also charted out the distance back to the crawlspace opening to the outside. Drew figured it would take him about six seconds to scoot on his back to the exit point. During that time, he could fire off eight more rounds. After that, he would be blind as to what was happening inside the house. He would have to rely on Gerardo and Chino to have made their way down the hill and in position to immediately respond to the gunfire.

Gerardo was lying face down in the dirt. Dirt, again, he thought. He was about twenty yards from the front door to the house. What was going to happen once the shooting started was anybody's guess. He knew he had to move fast and with lethal force. He was committed. There was no turning back.

For years he looked the other way as violence and death were inflicted upon others. Some deserving, others not. Gerardo stopped believing in God after witnessing violence and evil so extreme that no person could convince him a God existed who would allow it to occur. His mother would tell him it is a matter of faith, you had to believe. She told him that *El Señor* had a plan for us all, and sometimes it took a long time for it to present itself. Now, as he pulled the firearm from the back of his waistband with the understanding that he would be taking the lives of any number of men, he tried to imagine that maybe it was God's plan for him to be here. Right now, at this moment.

Nice try. No God, no purpose. Just some payback to some lawless *pendejos* who were about to have their lives cut short. But still, just maybe . . .

Chino saw it before Gerardo did. A set of headlights coming down from the right, on the same dirt access road. Fuck, more people with guns. He could make out an SUV, but he noticed a light package on top of the vehicle. Then as the vehicle came closer, he could notice that the vehicle had two-tone paint. Dark and light. Fucking cops. Border Patrol? As the vehicle came rolling up the driveway to the front of the house, Chino considered signaling to the vehicle but decided against revealing his position.

Something was wrong with this picture. The SUV was law enforcement; he could make out an insignia on the side of the driver's door. The men in front of the house did nothing to hide their automatic weapons. The SUV came to a leisurely stop in front of them. Two uniformed men got out of the SUV. Fucking Border Patrol, Chino swallowed his disgust. The men standing guard smiled and waved the officers forward.

"No. No. No!" Chino nearly screamed to himself. Dirty cops! Border Patrol, ICE, whatever. It didn't matter. This changed things. A shootout at the *narco* corral was a no harm, no foul thing. With law enforcement on the scene, there were two people whom they could not kill. And what a mess it would make after the shooting was over.

Chingada madre! Gerardo was watching the same thing transpire. *Pinche* dirty *migra!* Their presence was a major problem for their little search-and-destroy mission. Gerardo didn't have to wonder whether Chino saw the green and white U.S. Border Patrol SUV because it was parked right in front of the entrance to the house. The two officers who walked in did not have their guns drawn, and they were not investigating a crime. They were part of a crime.

If Drew did not see the officers enter the residence and began the shooting, Gerardo and Chino would have no choice but to enter and begin the battle. In a way, Gerardo thought, he shouldn't worry about what would happen to the officers. Life or death, his *abuela* used to tell him, was up to *la fortuna*. We had no control. But he had every bit as much a chance as dying as any man in the house and, in a way, he was every bit as deserving.

FORTY-TWO

Drew heard the door open and close above him. Heavy feet, two men. Combat boots, the footfalls were all too familiar. They crossed the floor and stood within five feet of Chance, who was not moving.

"Fuck, Caritas!" said one voice, clearly upset.

"The load trailer is still here," the other voice said. "The load is still here, I assume, and you're torturing some poor fuck for fun?"

"This *pinche gordo* and his friends," Caritas said angrily, "killed two of my men and came back here to kill more."

"Why would they do that?"

"Two reasons," Caritas was circling Chance as he spoke. "They know that we know who they are, and where they live."

Caritas stopped his pacing to admire the purple-black color of the blood caking on Chance's skull.

"What's the other?"

"Oh, yes," Caritas seemed to snap out of his daze, "and this concerns us all."

Caritas made his way over to the officers and stopped in front of them.

"They saw the load."

There was a silence for ten seconds.

"Where are they now?"

"Out there in the hills, no doubt," Caritas said, walked to the window, and pulled the curtain back.

"No," the man seemed upset. "The load. Where is the load?"

174

"They are still in the barn."

"We need to get them out of here and to the delivery spot."

Drew could not make out any features of the two men who were new to the scene. They spoke English without any accent, and they were some sort of military. But why would American military be here, Drew thought. He moved to the right of the widest gap in the floorboards to get a better view. The boots, more visible, looked to be military-grade black. Above the boot, he could see a dark green pant leg with a yellow stripe up the side.

The stripe answered his questions. Law enforcement. Motherfucking dirty law enforcement. A brand-new problem to deal with, and a whole new set of consequences.

"Listen," one of the men said to Caritas, "you can do what you want with these fuckers out in the hills, but we need to move the cargo. Lot of money on the line. We already accepted payment and transferred it to the vehicle."

"Looks to me like you are going to have to make a few people disappear," said the other man.

"*Claro que si*," Caritas said in agreement as he moved closer to Chance. "Make no mistake, they will be dealt with. I know where to find them."

"Well then deal with that shit and let's get this load out."

Chance began to move and let out a low, painful moan.

Caritas slapped Chance across the face with the back of his right hand.

"*Despierta! Pinche puto!*" Caritas shouted into Chance's blood-caked ear.

Drew could hear Chance coughing and spitting onto the floor.

"*Mira, Gordo*," Caritas said as he lifted Chance's face with the back of his hand, "just let me know where the others are, and I can end this pain for you."

Both of his eyes were swollen nearly shut, but Chance seemed to tilt one of them toward Caritas.

"I was wondering," Chance said and then spit more blood and mucus on the floor, "whether your mother knows that she gave birth to such a worthless sack of shit."

One of the men behind Caritas let out a small laugh but quickly silenced himself as Caritas turned around. Caritas walked over to the man and stopped in front of him. The man understood the nature of his disrespect and stood hunched over, eyes downcast. Caritas said nothing but reached with his hand to push the man's leather jacket to the side. He pulled out a knife that was sheathed on the man's waist. The knife had a silver handle with a ten-inch, serrated blade. Caritas examined the blade of the knife while the man continued to look down at the ground. The only sound in the room was Chance spitting blood onto the floor. Caritas ran his finger over the blade of the knife and then to the tip. He abruptly turned and walked back to Chance.

Chance lifted his head and tilted it to the right as if to get a better look out of his swollen left eye.

"Fucking do it already," Chance was gasping for breath, "I'm not telling you shit."

Caritas said nothing and stared at Chance for a few seconds. Without saying a word, he plunged the knife to the hilt into the gunshot wound in Chance's shoulder. Chance winced and screamed. The shriek was unnerving even to Caritas' men. At least one of them stepped back and looked away.

"Motherfucker, motherfucker!" Chance managed to say in a strangled breath. He was resigned to what was to come.

Caritas twisted the knife. The sound of the blade mashing flesh could be heard despite the renewed screams from Chance. He squirmed and writhed in his seat and uselessly tried to pull his shoulder away from the knife, which had pierced through his back near his shoulder blade.

Drew was below, speechless witness to torture. He would have to move soon and fast, he thought, because Chance could not last much longer. He looked to his right to chart his egress after the shooting started. He figured he would have about four seconds after the first person was hit until they figured out the rounds were coming from below. At that point, he surmised, he would have about eight angry *narcos* firing indiscriminately into the floor and, depending upon where he was, at him.

Drew determined which of the shoe soles above him belonged to Caritas so he could deliver a painful and confusing blow to the leader. For a moment, he tossed around the idea of trying to hit him in the testicles, but the bullet might ricochet through the floorboards and miss him. Drew needed the first round to be decisive. Barrel to the floorboard, he thought, that's the only way it could go down.

Drew started to track the footfalls of Caritas as he moved around Chance. Drew slid his body to a point about two feet in front of where Chance was tied to the chair. From this vantage point, Drew could see a bit better through a one-eighth-inch gap in the floorboard. He pulled the firearm up to the floorboard gap, grasping the handle with both hands.

"*Mira, Gordo,*" Caritas now stood directly in front of Chance, "*yo pienso* that you do not want to live out the rest of your soon-to-be-short life in agonizing pain knowing that I am personally going to find your family and fuck them up for your own stupidity." Caritas reached down with the knife he had yanked out of Chance's shoulder and wiped blood and tissue off the blade on Chance's shirt.

Chance could only look up. Although he wanted to speak, the words could not form in his mouth. Chance dropped his chin to his chest and looked down at the floor. Caritas smirked at the resignation on Chance's face. He noticed a few of his men mumbling and moving about. Caritas took a step away from Chance as if to get a better view of the carnage.

"*Bueno, pues,*" he said tapping the knife blade on the palm of his left hand, "I gave you a—"

A bright flash lit the room, and a distorted boom followed. Caritas folded over and collapsed to the floor with a high-pitched scream. Blood splashed across the ceiling as confused men tried to comprehend what was happening around them. An instant later, the unmistakable sound of gunfire permeated the room. Men ran to the window or dropped to the floor. When the face of one of the men lying on the floor peeled back in a ferocious eruption, some of the men realized gunfire was coming from below them. A few started to fire into the floorboards while dancing precariously around the room, trying to avoid being hit. At the same time, windows blew out on both sides the house from gunfire.

Caritas was on the floor holding his left leg up from his calf. A bullet had torn through his foot. The slip-on nightclub shoe had been blown off, exposing a pulpy, bloody mess.

Confused men continued to fire in all directions. Smoke and the pungent odor of gunpowder filled the room. Drew was able to fire off four rounds before the first shot came bursting through the floorboards. He rolled toward the exit and fired every time his body faced up. The pistol grip felt warm and powerful in his hands. Drew felt almost at home with the familiar chemical smell and smoke filling the crawlspace. Even in the chaos, Drew found himself to be composed and deliberate. He kept an eye on the floor above him to watch for movement. He figured he could get off about four more rounds before he reached the exit opening but then he would be out. He would have to make each shot count. Maybe he could pick up another firearm when he got outside. Drew was rolling and firing when he heard Chino's unmistakable voice.

"Alamo! Alamo!"

***

Chino felt the warm rush of familiarity when he heard the first shot from the house. He could feel blood pulse through his veins and his body go into automatic combat mode. The muscles and ligaments in his legs and arms fired like electric charges as he sprang to his feet and began his sprint to the house. He leveled his firearm in front of him as he unloaded two quick rounds into the window by the front door. He knew that would cause confusion and allow him to get closer without being fired on.

He heard four more rounds being fired with a muffled, wood-splitting thud. Rolling onto the porch of the house, he came to a rest below the window to the right of the front door. Looking up from the ground he could see at least two men were standing by the window with guns drawn looking for something to shoot. He could hear the screaming inside the house. At least a few men had been hit.

Time to fuck shit up.

Chino could see the surprise on the two men at the window as he sprang into their view. Without pause, he fired a round into each of their heads. He had seen blood before, but there was something momentarily intoxicating watching the spray back as the bodies fell. It was then that he could get a clear view of the interior room.

Caritas was lying on his side holding his bent leg. His foot was a gruesome wreck, and the mangled shreds were visible across the room. Four men, two in law enforcement uniforms, were standing and firing into the floor. Chino pointed at one of the uniformed men and hesitated. It was the uniform. Part of Chino knew he shouldn't be shooting U.S. agents. The other part managed to snap him out of his fog as he saw the man swing a firearm his way.

At that instant, he saw the back door burst open and Gerardo barreled in low and fired at the standing men. The man who had been pointing his gun at Chino was distracted for an instant, and Chino let off two rounds in quick succession. The man in the uniform went down with a chest wound about four inches below his neckline. He screamed out and fell back against the wall with blood pulsating over the hand he pressed against the gaping hole.

Two more rounds came crashing through the floorboards, and Chino knew Drew was still underneath. Drew had hit the other Border Patrol officer up through the right thigh and upper arm. He went down in a spurting crimson heap and was screaming. The blood gushed out of the exit wound in his upper thigh.

"You assholes are dead!" He was holding his thigh and staring at Chino.

Chino sensed that things were getting out of control.

"Alamo! Alamo!" he yelled more as a command than in fear.

"I know who you are, you fuck," the officer on the floor bellowed at Chino, "and you are—"

"*Chinga tú madre*," Gerardo said as he took two steps over to the man and fired into his head.

Thin white smoke from all of the gunshots pooled low throughout the small room. Chino looked around to see six dead men lying in increasingly larger pools of blood. He could see one man sprawled face down at the threshold of the front door. Caritas was alive and writhing in the corner holding what was left of his right foot. One uniformed Border Patrol officer in the corner with his hand over the hole in his chest, but he would bleed out in minutes. He sat there with a vacant gaze as blood streamed out around his hand. Chance was still slumped in his chair, bleeding from his shoulder and right leg, but alive.

"Gather the weapons," Chino motioned to Gerardo.

Gerardo didn't move. His gaze was fixed on something behind Chino, who turned and saw another man in a Border Patrol uniform. He was bound and gagged. Duct tape across his mouth and wrapped around the top half of his torso as if he were a mummy. The man had been beaten, and his right eye was swollen to the size of a fist. His other eye was open, looking in the direction of Chino and Gerardo with unmistakable fear.

Gerardo began to gather handguns from the dead men and toss them to the center of the room. He picked up the Tec9 and saw that the ammo clip was missing. He decided that they didn't have time to search the cars or dead bodies to look for ammunition. He tossed it off behind the couch. As he passed Caritas, Gerardo gave him a gratuitous kick to the ribs.

"*Pinche llorón!*" Gerardo followed the rib kick with a pistol whip to Caritas' pulpy foot.

Caritas screamed out in agony.

"You fuckers are all dead!"

Gerardo saw the knife that Caritas had been using on Chance on the floor and kicked it over to Chino.

"We'll see about that, *pendejo.*" Gerardo continued to move about the room sweeping for weapons until he made his way back to Chance.

"Where's Drew?" Chino asked Gerardo.

Looking down at the wood floor damaged by the rounds coming up from under the house, Gerardo could see that they made a line to the exterior wall.

"I am guessing that he made his way out to the barn and trailer," Gerardo said.

"*Órale, Gordo,*" he said moving to cut the duct tape around his hands with a knife. "Good to see you again."

Chance looked up through his one good eye and gave him a nod.

"Sorry," he said, coughing up blood.

"No need, Gordo," Gerardo said. "You did good, real good."

Chino moved to the bound and gagged man in uniform and removed the duct tape from around his mouth. The ripping sound of the duct tape being removed caused Gerardo to look up over Chance's shoulder.

"Who . . ." the man was gasping for air, "Who are . . ."

Chino knew from experience that every battle plan had unexpected twists. The discovery of this hostage was one of them. This man witnessed the entire incident and had seen all their faces. Still, he thought, this man clearly was not one of them. He was bound and gagged and, Chino guessed, would have been executed. Chino placed his hand on the man's shoulder and spoke slowly and clearly.

"Listen to me very carefully. You are going to be all right. The less you know about us, the better. Just know that we are on your side, and that you are going to come out of this alive. Do you understand me?"

The man nodded and made it clear he understood.

Chino looked around at the carnage. Dead men on the floor. Dead law enforcement. Blood everywhere. Gerardo had torn off a bed sheet from the window and was pressing it into the bloody hole in Chance's shoulder. He figured that the man had only seconds to get a real good look at any of them and he had not seen Drew. He walked into the kitchen for a dish towel.

"Look I know you are not going to like this, but I am going to have to blindfold you now, so remember what I told you," Chino tried to sound reassuring. "You are going to live through this. Are we cool?"

The man nodded.

"We've got us a little problem," Chino said while holding the tied-up officer by the collar.

"*Chingada madre!*" Gerardo said as he stood over Caritas.

"You have a bigger problem than that," Caritas said with a smirk as he looked up from the ground holding his wounded leg.

FORTY-THREE

Drew counted at least twelve rounds fired inside the house as he wriggled out of the crawlspace. He heard Chino and knew he was inside. Drew got up in a low crouch and ran to the barn. The side door was locked with a deadbolt. Drew moved farther down and found a window with a dark shade drawn. He bashed the window with the butt of his gun and was able to reach in and unlatch the window.

He noticed he could no longer hear any gunfire. Men were dead, he thought. He couldn't know whether it was his friends or Caritas and crew. Either way, he was committed, all in, to get to the children.

As he was crawling in through the window opening, Drew could hear whimpering. The interior was dark and smelled of animal urine, dried grass, and motor oil. It made him gag. The room was almost pitch black; all the windows had been covered with black paint. He headed along the wall toward the front door, running his hand along the wall searching for a light switch.

Drew felt a switch and flipped it on. The overhead fluorescent lights were blinding and harsh. Drew needed a moment to adjust his eyes. He looked down at the floor to adjust his focus. When he looked up, Drew could see them. Six boys and six girls, all lined up and seated against the far wall of the barn. They looked to be between the ages of six and eight years old. Each was bound at the wrist with a plastic zip tie. They were bound together from the wrists again in twos, again in zip ties. A long, heavy rope ran the length of the children, weaving between the bound hands and secured to eye hooks at opposite walls. He was silent as he took in the sight. He had not been prepared to see children bound like prisoners. These were the same zip ties he had used on detained combatants in Afghanistan. These were children in the United States, not much different in age than his own.

Drew's momentary trance was broken, and he moved slowly to the children. He noticed a set of gardening shears hanging on the far wall and went over to grab them. The children were not moving. The smell of urine was stronger as he came nearer to them as he could see several had wet their clothes or were sitting in a wet ring. The girl nearest him, maybe seven years old with big, deep brown eyes, looked up at him and whimpered, "*hambre.*" Drew understood enough to know she was hungry.

"It's okay," Drew said, emphasizing the okay, hoping it meant the same thing in Spanish as it did in English.

He began to cut zip ties off the children one by one. None of them moved after he cut the ties. Drew noticed that some children were more conscious than others.

"I'm going to get help," Drew said, holding his palms out, signifying for them to stay seated. "I will be right back." He emphasized each word as if slowing them down would make them more understandable to these terrified children.

Drew turned, checked the clip on his firearm and went out the door.

FORTY-FOUR

"*Pinche* motherfucking *putos!*" Caritas was screaming as Gerardo dragged him across the floor to the door.

Gerardo had just delivered a kick to his ribs when Drew came in through the back door with his gun drawn at the ready. For a moment, no one said a word. Drew surveyed the scene. Several men down on the floor, blood collecting in a pool in the middle. Another man with a hole in his chest sat on the floor propped against the wall, eyes open and lifeless. He was relieved to see his team still alive, although Chance looked like he had been in a car accident. His face was caked with blood, right eye swollen shut, and his shoulder looked to be field dressed with a massive amount of silver duct tape. He also noticed another man with a blindfold seated on the ground behind Chino.

"Everyone good?" Drew asked the group.

"Everyone except this motherfucker," Chance said as he drove his heel into Caritas' mangled foot.

Caritas screamed, the pain searing through his voice. "You fuckers are going to die. You, your kids, your friends, your—"

Gerardo gave a soccer style kick to Caritas' face, and he was out. For a moment, they all stood looking at Caritas on the floor, a group understanding of the significance of their situation. The one man who posed the most significant danger to them was still alive. The problem was clear. It was one thing to kill a man in a firefight but an entirely different thing to execute a man in cold blood.

"Drew," Chino said as walked over to Drew. "We've got a situation here."

"Fuck that," Chance said from a bent-over stance, hands on his knees and spitting up blood, "we need to waste this fucker!"

"You going to do it?" Drew asked.

Chance did not respond and looked over to Gerardo.

"The smart thing to do," Gerardo said, "is to put a bullet in this piece of shit and get the fuck out of here."

The others had no response.

"This *narco* junior has been torturing and killing people like he was playing a video game since he was eighteen and his uncle let him take over the operation," Gerardo said slowly, almost as if to justify it to himself. "And he will continue to kill and torture, make new widows and fatherless children until someone kills him."

Drew considered it but knew that assassinating an unconscious man was a line he was not willing to cross.

"Look," he said, "no one is going to put a bullet in his head. We need to figure something out. We also need to get those kids out of the barn and to safety.

"Fuck, Drew," Chino said as he started to kick the guns from the dead men to the center of the floor. "We've got nine bodies, two of them are dirty Border Patrol officers in fucking uniform, one mangled piece of shit cartel fuckhead, and a barn full of illegal alien kids tied up like prisoners of war. What the fuck are we supposed to do?"

"Not like we can call the cops." Chance added.

"I know what you can do."

The voice came from behind Chance and Drew. The man with the blindfold over his head.

"Who's that?" Drew asked.

"I am Border Patrol Agent Hector—"

He was cut off when the squelch of a radio phone that was lying on the ground went off. The unmistakable sound of the connection and the voice on the other.

"*Llegamos en unos quantos minutos.*"

Drew did not have to speak Spanish to know someone was going to be there in a few minutes.

"We need to bolt, NOW!" Chino said, gathering the firearms.

"What about this fuck?" Chance asked as he spit blood on Caritas.

"We have to take him with us," Drew said and turned to look out the window.

"Fuck that!" Chance reached down to pick up one of the handguns. "We need to waste this piece of shit."

No one responded. Chance walked over to Caritas with the gun in his hand.

Gerardo stopped Chance by placing a hand on his shoulder.

"*Mira, Gordo,*" Gerardo said, "your friend Drew is right. It's one thing to shoot at someone shooting at you. It's a whole different thing to kill them straight out."

"You were ready to waste the guy a few seconds ago!"

Gerardo paused to consider the option.

"This is the type of life I left behind," Gerardo said as he looked down at Caritas' unconscious body, "and let me tell you that you don't want to go there and I don't want to go back."

"Yeah, Chance," Chino chimed in, "I want to put a gun in his hand, wait for him to wake up and then blow his brains out, but wasting him like this . . ."

"No choice, boys," Drew said. "We take him with us."

Chance was having trouble standing and dropped to his knees with his hands on the ground. He spit up more blood. Chino walked over to help him back up.

"I got you buddy," Chino said pulling him up. "You did real good today."

"No shit," said Drew, "you never broke, you handled yourself like a stone cold badass!"

"Well," Gerardo added, "time to figure out our next move."

"Look," the man with the blindfold interjected. "I don't know you guys, haven't seen any of you enough to get a positive ID. But I know you all saved my life, and that is worth a whole lot of shit to us. You saved me from a couple of dirty officers and their crime partners. Let me out of this, and I can help you. I know it will be a fucking shitstorm, but I can help."

"What do you think, boss?" Chino asked Drew.

"I think that we need to move. We need to get these kids out of here before the rest of these fucks show up. We can deal with this on the move. Chino, put the officer with you in the truck and trailer."

"Copy that."

"Chance," Drew said, "you play clean up here. Gather up all the weapons, don't leave any behind."

"I'm on it."

"Gerardo, you're with me, we need to get the kids into the trailer."

"Ándale, pues," Gerardo nodded to Drew.

Drew went outside to the crawlspace entry. He returned with the bottle of gasoline that he had placed there before he entered and the shooting started. He tossed the bottle to Chino.

"Torch the house," he said.

"Copy that, boss."

"Wait, wait," the officer said as Gerardo was helping him up, "if you guys aren't going to take this thing off my head . . ."

He paused for a second.

". . . and I am pretty sure, pretty hopeful that you are not going to put a bullet in my head."

He had all their attention.

"Would you please stop using your names around me."

FORTY-FIVE

Gerardo stopped dead when he entered the barn. They were all still seated, bound at the wrist in twos and connected to one long rope. The children were quiet, but several were sobbing. He focused on the boy and girl he had spoken to in the journey across the desert. He couldn't tell if they remembered him as they sat motionless with blank gazes.

"Drugged," Gerardo said as he approached the children.

"Yeah," Drew said. "they are all pretty out of it."

The zip ties had been cut but the children were still bound together by a rope at the waists.

"Probably best to keep them tied together until we get them in the trailer," Gerardo said motioning with his hand to the long rope connecting them. "That would make it easier getting them all in."

Drew made his way over to the workbench and picked up the shears he used earlier to cut the ties on the kids' wrists.

"Right," Drew said, handing Gerardo the shears. "Let's get them all in the trailer. You get in the back with them and then start cutting the ropes."

Gerardo nodded and in a soothing voice he told the children he and the others were there to save them.

"*No tengan miedo*," Gerardo told them.

Drew left the barn to fire up the truck and reattach the trailer.

"*Ahora*," Gerardo said to the children, "everybody up." He motioned with his hand for them to stand. As they began, to stand it struck Gerardo as sad that even in this drugged and traumatized state the children responded to orders as if they had been doing it all of their short lives.

When they were all on their feet, he led them out of the barn and to the trailer. Drew had the rear door open and the ramp was down for the children to climb in. Off to his right, he could see Chino and Chance. Chino was dragging Caritas by the back collar of his shirt. The shirt was pulling up from his stomach, and Caritas was screaming. Chino pulled Caritas up from the ground and shoved him into the back seat of one of the SUVs parked by the barn. Chino swung into the driver's seat, and Chance got into the back seat with Caritas. Chance sat with his back to the side window, pointing his handgun at Caritas.

Gerardo did his best to keep talking to the children as he sat them down on the floor of the trailer. Drew came up from behind him.

"Are we good to go?"

"As good as we are going to be."

Chino stepped out of the SUV and walked over to the truck.

"Hey, boss," Chino wiped the sweat off his brow with the back of his hand, "where the fuck are we going?"

Drew couldn't respond sensibly. He looked out into the desert night and knew he could not begin to understand the clusterfuck he had started and must somehow see to a finish.

"The fuck away from here." That was all he could manage.

"Sounds like somewhere that I want to be right about now," Chino said as he turned to trot back to the SUV.

Chino climbed in and started the engine. Chance did not break his gaze on Caritas.

"What's the plan, Chino?" he asked.

"The plan is to get as far as fuck away from here and," he said, "stay the fuck alive."

"That's not going to happen, you *putos*," Caritas said, the words coming through his clenched teeth, "You fuckers are gonna die."

Without saying a word, Chance struck Caritas across the face with the barrel of his gun. More blood gushed from Caritas' face.

"You motherfucker," Caritas said, his face turned away from Chance. "I should have cut the ears off your fat head."

Chance said nothing. Instead, he moved closer to Caritas and drove his foot down on Caritas' mangled foot. Caritas screamed long and loud. Chance continued to turn his foot to inflict more pain. Chance wished he was wearing some of those *narco* cowboy boots instead of his stupid high tops.

Chino watched from the rearview mirror and said nothing. This fucker deserved the pain. And death. That was yet to be determined.

Drew started up the truck, which produced a deep and powerful roar. At least these smuggler assholes knew enough to get powerful vehicles. The thought was lost as he saw the movement of light against the night sky. Someone was coming fast.

Drew stepped on the gas and sped down the center of the dirt road toward the mountain ahead of him.

FORTY-SIX

Drew drove ahead of Chino. Headlight beams were the only illumination, making driving difficult and slow. Drew assumed it was worse for Chino because he would also have to contend with Drew's dust cloud. The road curved into the night, and Drew was distracted when his dash lights caught the unmistakable shape of a gun handle sticking out from underneath the passenger side seat. Just then, a severe jolt shook Drew up out of the seat. He lost control of the steering wheel for a second and the truck veered to the right. The trailer swerved left. The fishtail caused the right side of the truck to lift off the ground. He regained control of the wheel, but the truck came to an abrupt stop, and the engine quit. The harsh stop sent Drew hard into the seatbelt harness. He leaned back against the seat and looked out his driver's side window. He could see that Chino was moving slowly his way.

Drew reached down to turn the key on the ignition. The engine turned over quickly, but as he put the truck into gear, he could feel the left rear tire spinning and the truck would not move. The trailer had slid to the left of the dirt road, and its rear wheels were suspended two feet above a slope. The weight of the trailer lifted the rear of the truck tires so that the wheels were not touching the ground.

"Fuck! Fuck! Fuck!" Drew roared. He slammed his fist on the steering wheel.

Looking back, Drew could see the lights coming on. Chino was already out of his truck and running over.

"We got company, boss," Chino was shouting as he made it to Drew's window.

"I know. I know," Drew jumped out of the truck and sped back to the trailer. Drew was once again struck by the damp, musky smell that came rushing out the open door. The children were all now awake and alert. They had the startled look of children being tossed around inside a moving trailer. Four or five were crying. The others stared blankly off in space.

"Everybody out!" Drew yelled.

"*Vámonos, chicos!*" Gerardo chimed in and started escorting the children out.

"We're going to have to make a stand here," Drew said to Chino. "The trailer's fucked, and we can't leave these kids."

"I'll take the truck up the road and circle back for you on foot. Chance can keep an eye on the *narco* fuck."

"What's his status?" Drew asked.

"He's combat ineffective," Chino said, "but he hates that dude enough to keep a gun pointed at him and pull the trigger if he needs to."

Drew gave Chino a nod and surveyed the area. They had just come around a curve, and the road ahead had a bend to the right. Small rolling hills dotted with cactus and low mesquite were off to the left. To the right, flat, barren terrain, nowhere to hide. Drew looked over to Gerardo, who already had the children out and was corralling them near the hill side of the road.

"I'm taking them to the first hill," Gerardo said with one hand on the shoulder of a sobbing little girl. "If I can get them to calm down and stay put, I will come back down."

"No," Drew said, still looking down the road, "stay with them. These fuckers are not getting those kids."

"You can't face them alone. You don't know how many there are, how many guns. Gordo's out, and your amigo Chino may not make it back in time."

"I've got about eight rounds in this weapon," Drew pulled back the clip in his handgun, "and I saw another gun in the truck."

"You need to make every round count."

"That's what the Marines paid me to do."

"You could just come with me and these kids."

"No." Drew walked over to the truck and checked the clip on the gun from under the dash. "They'd only find us, and who knows what would happen."

Gerardo knew he was right. He reached behind and pulled out his handgun.

"Take it," Gerardo said. "I've got maybe five rounds left."

"You keep it. You just may need every round if things go bad for us," Drew said and held up the gun he found in the truck. "Nine rounds in this one. Plus, eight in the other."

Drew tucked the gun from the truck in the back of his waistband. "That's plenty to inflict a lot of damage in close quarters."

Gerardo smiled. "Let's just hope there are not eighteen of them."

"Then I'll line up two of these assholes for one shot."

Gerardo laughed. "What if there are nineteen?"

"Then somebody is going have a broken neck."

Gerardo gave him a nod and returned to the children, who were near hysteria. He did his best to calm them.

"We're taking you to a safe place," he told them in a reassuring voice, "but I need everyone to listen to me and stay low."

None of the children responded.

"Please tell me that you understand what I am telling you."

A few of the children nodded and one, the boy with whom he made contact on the trail, moved forward and took Gerardo's hand.

Gerardo smiled at the boy and then looked up to the group.

"*Bueno*," he said, "let's get out of here."

***

Drew walked back up the road away from the truck. He surveyed the terrain for any places of active concealment. His wanted positions from which he could move quickly and covertly. He would use them once the shooting started if he had to move away from the firing zone. The road's bend to the right and the stalled truck and trailer would cause an oncoming car to make a quick stop. If the vehicle was moving fast enough, Drew thought, they might lock the brakes and come to a sliding halt. If that happened, he would be ready with a nice surprise.

Or not. If they saw the stalled vehicles and reacted, he would have to face them in the open road. He assessed the situation. Take random, possibly inaccurate shots from behind a hill or draw them in and beat them to the draw. Just like a western.

Still, standard protocol would be to look for safe routes of concealment if the shooting got spread out. Drew saw the left side of the bend was bordered by a low hill, about twenty feet high. He estimated the top of the hill to be about thirty yards from the center of the road. Even in the hands of an experienced sniper, handguns were not very accurate over distances. And many variables affected how accurately he could fire a weapon he did not maintain. Familiarity with the trigger pull, proper cleaning, and loading of the individual rounds to name a few. Imagining the vectors and lines of sight to his targets, Drew knew he would have to get closer if he were to prevail. He remembered what an instructor once told him about handguns. Most people would be more effective throwing a rock than accurately aiming and discharging a handgun. Still surveying the scene, at least knew one thing. He was not just most people. Whatever was about to happen, he knew once thing for certain. People were going to die.

***

Chino pulled the truck off the road about a quarter of a mile north of Drew. He knew he needed to get back ASAP to help Drew. He assessed the unknowns. The number of men coming down the road. The firepower. Their experience. He assessed what he knew. He had one bleeding junior *narco*, a bloody and barely conscious Chance, a federal officer whom he did not know and whom they had essentially kidnapped or rescued, depending on how you looked at it.

Firearm check. Chino popped the clip of the gun. Four rounds. One handgun on the floor of the driver's seat. How did that get there, he thought. Who cares, four more rounds.

"Chance," Chino pushed him by the shoulder to see if he was still conscious. "How many rounds in your gun?"

Chance squinted through the blood-caked eye that was not completely swollen shut.

"Looks like two."

"You guys fucked up, my men are taking no prisoners, Caritas said in almost singsong. "Except you my fat friend, I will save you to finish what I started."

Chance, sitting next to him in the back cab of the truck, cracked him across the bridge of the nose with the gun butt.

Caritas screamed out, his face now mashed.

"Just wait, *pendejo gordo*, I am . . ."

Chance delivered two more blows to his face and grabbed a dirty T-shirt off the floor of the cab and shoved it into Caritas' mouth.

"Two rounds." Chance was spitting blood as he spoke. "Enough to make sure this piece of shit does not see another day."

Barely able to breathe, Caritas slumped down and looked out the window into the darkness.

Chino moved over to the agent and took off the blindfold. The agent adjusted his eyes to interior light of the vehicle. Chino handed one of the handguns over to the agent.

"Okay, Johnny Law," he said in a measured pace, "you are just as dead as we are if this thing goes to shit, so you might as well have some sort of say in the outcome."

The agent reached for the weapon slowly.

"Ramirez," he said. "Border Patrol Officer Hector Ramirez."

Chino gave him a nod.

"Well, Ramirez," Chino stepped out of the vehicle, "if we make it out of this thing alive, maybe then we can figure out where we all stand."

Chino stood and spoke to the agent through the open door. "We cool?"

"Absolutely," Ramirez said as he checked the clip on the handgun. "Would be cooler with a few more rounds."

"You and me both. Let's go."

***

Gerardo herded the children up the slope of the hill and over the top, just out of sight.

"It's almost over," he said. "Everyone needs to stay quiet and not move."

He looked for understanding from the children, but all he could garner was the fear and confusion that kept them whimpering.

"I will not let anything happen to you," once again in a comforting voice, "*te lo prometo.*"

Gerardo considered his situation. They were about 100 yards from Drew and the trailer. The children were small and, now, dirt covered. None of them had on bright clothes. From a distance, if they stayed still, they were indiscernible in the dark from any low brush or boulder. If Drew was unsuccessful, he had a seventy-five percent chance that the smugglers would set off in a different direction in their hunt for the kids. That would give him a head start in the dark, and they would be moving low and fast. Of course, Gerardo thought, fleeing in the dark would mean Drew, Chino, and the Border Patrol agent were dead.

He looked back and the children, hunkered down and mostly silent. He knew the brutal truth. They were after the children. The children would not be killed, but they were headed off for a life of abuse and pain. If they found him, they would kill him, and that would be it. Face down in the dirt off a backroad in the desert foothills. *Pinche* dirt again. He couldn't avoid it. His life depended on what happened in the next few minutes.

FORTY-SEVEN

Drew stood to the right of the open door on the driver's side of the truck. The truck had stalled with the front of the cab veered slightly back to the road. The door was ajar, so he was able to place one of the guns in the door pocket. He had snuffed the dome light. The other gun was tucked deep into the back of his waistband. He figured he could get two or three shots off before ducking behind the open door and around the front of the truck. The trick was to get them close enough to be effective with the handgun. Once they came within view, he would have only seconds to act. He knew Chino would be in a place that had some strategic advantage. Their training would prevent him from coming out into the open and standing beside him like some old cowboy movie. At least he hoped that.

Drew heard movement from behind and turned in time to see Chino stepping into the road. Chino moved up beside Drew. So much for training.

"You didn't think I'd leave you out here by yourself?"

"I was kinda hoping you would." Drew kept his eyes on the road ahead of him. "But I knew you wouldn't."

Chino stood to the right of Drew. Once again, Drew scanned the perimeter for vantage points. The side of the road off to his right had some low mesquite brush and a few boulders and, in the dark, could provide some minimal coverage, not enough to stop a bullet.

"When the shooting starts, get low and make it to the brush," Drew said.

"We've got a friendly off to your right," Chino said but did not look in that direction, "about four o'clock."

"Copy that. I take it our Border Patrol agent has joined the fight."

"We had no choice. We're all in this deep shit together."

"Does he have a name?"

"Ramirez. His name is Ramirez."

"Well," Drew let out a subdued laugh, "it can't get any more FUBAR than this, so we might as well have a fed in our showdown."

Drew knew things were spinning out of control. He wasn't sure how many crimes he might have committed this evening, but he was sure of one thing. Making it out of this alive was more important than what might happen with the law.

"What's your plan, chief?" Chino asked.

"I'm working on it. But, like I said, when I make a move you go opposite of me to widen the target range. I'll be moving fast."

Drew reached back to reposition the butt of the gun in his waistband. "We're going to need to get them close to us to make these handguns effective. My guess is that these cowboys have no real firearm skills and will just be firing in this general direction."

"Well, let's make ours count."

"You know how to roll on this."

"Center mass those motherfuckers," Chino said, moving the butt of the gun closer to his right hip.

Only seconds later the first truck came into view, a dark vehicle with scorching bright search lamps high on the roll cage. Drew couldn't make out how many men were inside or whether any were riding in the bed of the truck. As the truck came to a stop, about forty yards from him, a dark SUV pulled up alongside. For about twenty seconds there was no movement from either of the vehicles.

Drew began to improvise. He stepped forward with both hands in the air, no weapon showing. Chino stepped up five feet to his right.

"Hey boss," Chino said almost in a whisper, "any tricks to that Jedi breathing thing you do?"

Drew smiled.

"Just think of it as clearing a machine. A deep breath and then push the distractions out with your exhale."

Drew could hear Chino start to draw a breath, and he started his own. The scent of the desert, dirt, and bittersweet plants filled his head and lungs. He pushed out the breath slowly, keeping an eye on the trucks. As the breath left his body, Drew felt focused again. He knew the task. No sense waiting around for something to happen.

"I am a Weapon, I am the Dark, I am the Silence, I am Death," Drew said in a low whisper.

Chino looked over at Drew and said nothing.

Drew started walking toward the vehicles.

Chino walked with him.

FORTY-EIGHT

Two men got out of the truck in front of Drew, and three came out of the SUV. Drew couldn't make out any facial features. They were men, and they were armed. One had a short-barreled rifle of some sort. Given their love of *narco* movies, Drew assumed it was an Uzi or Tec-9. The others had handguns. The priority target was the guy with the Uzi. The others would be laboring under the same difficulties as Drew and Chino, weapons that are ineffective at long range. Drew also assumed that none of these men had formal weapons training. Blowing off a hundred rounds in the desert at stationary beer cans hardly qualified them as expert marksmen. He could also assume they were not accustomed to dealing with individuals who were experienced with military tactics.

"You ready, Chino?"

"Right here, like always."

Drew continued walking, hands still in the air. Chino was now off to his right about two steps back but still walking forward. They came to within ten feet of the vehicles. Both vehicles had turned off the engines, and the headlights went off. The running lights remained illuminated on both vehicles.

Big mistake, Drew thought.

"*Alto, pendejos!*" A shout from the man facing Drew.

Drew did not say a word and kept his hands in the air. He could feel that familiar rush of adrenaline that danger created. The man with the submachinegun was in front of him. Drew could see the outline of the weapon. It was an Uzi. He reached back in his memory and found a hazy recollection that an Uzi had at least a thirty-two-round magazine. Given the accelerated firing capacity per minute, the shooter could fire for about four seconds before he had to reload. He noticed the man had the weapon slung facing down at his waist. His left hand held the receiver, and his right was on the hand guard. He couldn't tell for sure, but Drew figured that the position of the hand meant that his finger was on the trigger. He could see he was wearing tight jeans, a polo shirt, and baseball hat. Nothing about his clothing or stance indicated military training. The one standing on the other side of the vehicle facing him had tucked his handgun into his waistband with the butt exposed. His posture was that of the leader, seemingly assured that those behind him had their weapons drawn for support. The three off to his right facing Chino were gathered around the other vehicle. One stepped forward in front of the SUV. Drew could not see a gun in his hand or on his person. He wore jeans, western-style boots and a cowboy hat. His collared shirt strained to enclose his girth. The other two stayed by the open driver- and passenger-side doors. Drew noticed they were wearing khaki cargo-style pants and tactical boots. Each had his weapon drawn, two hands holding the firearm in a locked position. These two had military or law enforcement training, Drew reasoned.

Uzi man would have to be first. Drew figured that hitting him would cause him to fire the weapon into the ground, which might make him lose control of the weapon. In any event, the gun that could do the most damage would be neutralized for a moment. If he did this, he would have to move right while firing, which meant Chino would have the two experienced gunmen to himself. The wildcard was Agent Ramirez. Drew knew nothing about the man. His experience, his courage or his willingness to engage in a gun battle were all unknowns.

"Where is the *patrón*?" asked the man out front in a heavy accent.

"We have him, and we are not giving him up until we reach a place of safety." Drew kept his eyes on the Uzi. Still pointing down.

"What makes you think that you can make it out of here." He laughed and was looking back at the two with the weapons drawn. "We know who you are, we know where you live."

Drew was thinking he was getting particularly tired of that phrase when Chino began to laugh. At first a snicker and then loud, boisterous blast.

"What is so funny to you, *pocho pendejo*?"

Chino looked over to Drew. It was the look between friends who knew each other from the inside out. No words needed to be exchanged, no turning back. Go time.

"You know," Chino said, his hands now down on his hips, "I was thinking the same thing."

"The same thing?"

"Yeah." Chino could sense the presence of the border agent behind him off to his right. "I was thinking what makes you fuckers think you are going to make it out of here alive."

That shut them up. Maybe they were translating Chino's words, but Drew could see the expression on the one with Uzi change. Just then a loud crack that sounded like breaking wood. Drew surmised it the Border Patrol agent behind him. He saw all the men look in the direction of the noise. This was his opportunity.

Drew fired first. His fake negotiating ploy had left him no choice but to hide his gun in the waistband at his back, something he usually would consider a disastrous tactic, but he made it work. He whipped his hand behind his back, pulled the weapon, and fired immediately. He could not tell if he hit the man but, as expected, the Uzi fired into the ground in an uncontrolled burst. Drew dropped to the ground to lower his profile. As the man brought up the Uzi, Drew shot him in the chest. Even in the dark, Drew could see the arterial spray from the chest wound spreading out and up. Drew assumed the others were firing their weapons, but he was in a tunnel, seeing and hearing only what was in front of him.

Drew swung his weapon left and began a sweep of the targets in front of him. The one man opposite of the Uzi had retreated behind the SUV door and was using the open door as protection. Drew could hear the unmistakable whiz and snap of bullets flying past him as the man fired at him. Drew rolled to his left and, when he righted himself, instinctively fired two rounds at the legs he could barely make out below the door. Drew saw him go down but start to move further behind the SUV.

Chino fired three quick shots as soon as he heard Drew fire. The second shot hit the one in front, the man who was doing the talking. It was a direct hit to the man's neck. The slug's impact knocked him off his feet and unleashed a blood fountain. Chino knew he had to move fast. He crouched low and ran twenty yards to his left. He could feel bullets disturbing the air all around him. One came close enough to his ear that he could feel heat. He stopped, dropped to one knee and fired back at the two still standing. Even from a distance of only fifteen feet, targets were difficult to make out in the darkness. He saw a muzzle flash and fired at it. He saw a figure drop to the ground. The one left standing started to move behind the vehicle, firing erratically. They were definitely not trained, which made Chino more confident as he dropped to his stomach and fired from the ground. He could hear Drew firing, but it looked like they were now in a standoff with two men still standing and protected by the vehicles.

Drew was still low to the ground and not firing, waiting for a target. He had forgotten how many rounds he had and realized he left one handgun back in the truck. This was not good.

"Chino!" Drew yelled. "We're fucked here. Advance on my move!"

"Copy that!"

Chino was hoping their new Border Patrol friend was listening.

"Flanking!" came a voice from behind the SUVs.

Drew knew Ramirez would move behind their opponents, and it was time for the final push.

"On me, Chino!"

The men were still firing from behind the SUV, but they were firing blindly into the night. Drew sensed they were confused and a little scared.

He cleared his mind, took in a deep breath and let it out slowly. Now or never, he thought. He got up, still low, and moved quickly to his right toward the opposite side of the SUV in front of him.

Chino made a break directly at the shooter and the SUV, blasting away as he ran. From behind the SUVs, Agent Ramirez came out the brush and began to fire at the men. The one shooting at Drew spun to see he was taking rounds from the rear. At that moment, Drew came around the side of the SUV to find he had a clear shot at the man who had turned toward Ramirez. Drew delivered two shots to the shooter's head from about five feet. As they exploded through the top of the man's skull, the rounds pushed out a salvo of hair, brains, and blood before the body fell limp to the ground. Drew rotated his aim to the gangster shooting at Chino and fired. Nothing.

"Fuck! I'm out!" Drew yelled.

Chino had moved to within ten feet of the man and was firing through the glass of the door that he was using for protection.

Drew watched helplessly. He froze. The shooter wielded his gun, pointed it at him. Time slowed. Drew could actually see the face of the shooter. Goatee. Graying at the bottom. A New England Patriots hat. Fuck, he hated the Patriots. Dark, marble eyes.

Out the corner of his eye, Drew saw Ramirez run up behind the man, stopping about five feet away. From a professional stance, both arms extended, Ramirez delivered a triple tap into the man's back.

The jolt of shots turned the man into a ragdoll. Both arms went out and up. The weapon flew out of his hands, and he went face down into the dirt.

The sudden end to the firing created an eerie silence. Drew could smell the sulfur signature of expended rounds. Moving forward toward the downed men, he came within view of Chino and Ramirez. No one said anything. Drew's heart raced, and his head pounded from adrenaline. He filled his lungs and slowly exhaled.

It was over.

FORTY-NINE

Gerardo could hear the shots below. Some of the children cried out in fear, others remained motionless and dazed. The firing lasted less than twenty seconds, but Gerardo knew there were dead men on the road. His choices were simple. Make his way down to the road and hope that his friends, if that is what you could call them, had been successful. The other choice was to run. Get the children up and start moving low and fast. If his side was dead then going now would give them a head start in the dark, moving away from the men below, some of whom might be wounded. He looked around him at the children. They were scared, tired, thirsty, and covered in dirt.

"*Puta madre*," he said to himself in a whisper, "I'm tired of running."

He looked at the children with both hands out, palms flat, in a calming gesture.

"Nobody move from here, no matter what," he said a forceful but low tone. "I will be back with help."

Gerardo turned and made his way back down the hill.

***

Chance weaved in and out of consciousness but the firing snapped him back into the present. Caritas was still unconscious from the last gun butt to the face that he gave him to stop the incessant whining about how they were all dead, we know where you live, yeah, yeah.

Fuck it, he thought. Let's put an end to this shit.

The gunfire gave him a second wind. Chance unbuckled the Caritas' belt, a big gold Gucci buckle. Typical *narco* bullshit style. He pulled the belt off and lashed it in a loop as tight as he could around Caritas' wrists behind his back. The pain in his shoulder pulsated with every movement. He pulled the long end through the steering wheel and brought it back to a tight knot leaving only about six inches between Caritas' bound wrists and the steering wheel. He leaned back in his seat, breathing hard, waiting for the wave of pain to subside. Chance double checked the bind. Tight on both ends. No chance of loosening. As he swung his leg out the vehicle, a pain shot again through his entire body. Everything hurt as his foot contacted the ground. The jersey he wore was soaked through with blood, and the hole in his shoulder was bleeding through the makeshift rag and duct tape bandage. Surveying the field dressing, he adjusted the wad under the duct tape. Not quite sterile, he thought, but, fuck it, I'm alive. Chance chambered his firearm and began to limp down the road.

***

"Holy motherfuck!" Chino said out loud as he surveyed the scene.

"You good, Chino?" Drew asked as he made his way over to him.

"I think so, but the truth is I don't know if I shit my pants or not."

"You good?" Drew nodded toward the agent.

"Looks like I'm okay."

All three stood numbly for a few seconds, but all of them heard movement in the brush off to the side of the road. All three pointed guns in the general direction of the noise.

"I was kind of hoping it was going to be you guys pointing a gun at me when I got down here." Gerardo walked out of the dark with his hands up.

"Fuck," Chino said, "I've never been so happy to see another Mexican in my life."

"You and me both, *carnal.*"

Gerardo stopped a few yards short of the group and looked behind Drew down the road.

"Now that is either the slowest-moving *narco* coming toward us or our very own Gordo." Gerardo laughed as he watched the unmistakable body shape of Chance hobbling down the road.

"Looks like we all made it," Drew said, easing out a long breath.

Chino walked over and put his arm around Drew's shoulder.

"Sure does look like it, boss."

FIFTY

While Gerardo headed up the hill to get the children, the rest made their way back to the truck where Caritas was still bound and unconscious. As the children came within view, Drew could see how young they were. They looked scared, confused, and unsure of whom to trust. Gerardo sat them all down and walked over to the truck.

"So," Chino said with a sweeping gesture of his arm, "we've got about five dead alien smugglers and their head honcho tied up in the truck, right?"

Chino looked over to the children. "Not to mention a pack of underage kids, drugged and tired in the middle of the fucking desert."

"Don't forget two dead federal agents," Drew said.

"Dirty federal agents!" Ramirez said.

"And let's not forget all the other bodies in the burning house."

No one said a word.

"Now what?" Chino asked.

Chance was in too much pain to even understand the gravity of the situation, and Drew's main concern was seeing his family before he was hauled off to jail.

"Let me tell you what I see here," Agent Ramirez said, his tone serious but measured. He had no trouble getting their attention.

"The dead agents, fuck those guys. They were working with these smugglers and were going to let . . ." Ramirez choked up, ". . . them kill me."

Ramirez scanned the faces of the men.

"Which is what they were going to do until . . ." he paused for a moment, "until you cowboys came to the rescue."

Drew started to say something but stopped when he saw Ramirez was not finished.

"Now, I don't know who you guys are, but I know that you are not with these assholes." Ramirez gestured with his head toward the bodies of the traffickers.

"You all saved my life," Ramirez said and tried to control a tear. "Because of you, I will be seeing my wife and three kids today."

Ramirez looked around the scene and then into the eyes of the men standing before him.

"I don't know what you all have been through in your lives. But nothing can prepare you for knowing that someone is going to end your life in matter of minutes."

Drew started to say something but Ramirez held out his open to hand to show that he was not finished.

"I was going to die. While I was in that house, bound and gagged," Ramirez now began to tear up, "all I could think of was the misery that my family...my kids would be going through for the weeks or months it would take to find my body somewhere out in the middle of this desert."

Ramirez took a breath and looked up as if to imagine the fallout to his family.

"But it was you guys," he looked at each one them, "that are giving my kids their father back."

There was silence between them for a few seconds.

"At least something good came of this," Drew said.

"Something good? Something good?" Ramirez was incredulous. "There are a bunch of innocent little kids here who will not," he looked at each of them, "I repeat, will not be peddled off to some degenerate pedophile for God knows what type of abuse."

"Copy that shit," Chino said with a touch of pride.

"Like I said, I owe you guys my life, so this is the way this is going down."

"This is a lot of shit to explain," Drew said.

"Well, it goes something like this. I was being held captive by these *narco* human-trafficking fucks after my partners turned on me. They had been working with them for months, and just by chance, I came upon their ranch while I was patrolling. I knew things were bad when they disposed of my vehicle." Ramirez paused at the thought. "They were set to kill me when you fine gentlemen came storming in like the fucking Navy SEALs . . ."

"Marines!" Chino said.

". . . Anyways, this was clearly a rip-off by a rival gang. I was beaten and so bloody everyone thought that I was dead. This gang— you—tied up *narco* junior, and a few of his men made a break from the house and fled down the road. You all," Ramirez pointed at them, "hightailed it out after them and had the shootout at the OK Corral."

"Why did this rival gang of mine leave the kids?" Drew asked.

"Kids? They didn't give a shit about any the kids." Ramirez looked surprised. "They were after the money."

"The money?" Chino perked up.

"What money?" Drew said.

215

"You guys weren't here for the money?" He searched their faces.

"Holy shit!" Ramirez laughed. "You guys really are the good guys. You came to save the kids."

"Fuck yes," Drew said, "but you don't want to know how all this started."

Drew looked over to Chino.

"Once we figured out what they were going to do with these kids we knew what we had to do. So, no this was not about any money, no kids were going to peddled off on our watch."

Chino was still dumbfounded. "Money? What money are you talking about?"

Ramirez laughed again.

"Well, forgive me if I wasn't taking copious notes when these fuckers were getting ready to murder my ass," Ramirez said. He started to walk over to the truck where Caritas remained bound and unconscious.

"But this pretty boy asshole was bitching to these guys as to why they couldn't pack $500,000 in a nicer bag . . ."

Ramirez stopped talking as he rummaged in the back-cab area of the truck.

". . . than this piece-of-shit duffel."

Ramirez held up a canvas green, overstuffed bag.

"What . . . what . . ." Chance started to say as he squinted through his swollen eye.

"What are we going to do with that?" Chino asked.

"Well," Ramirez said handing the bag to Drew, "I'm not a vain man, but I value my life with my family way more than $500,000." He smiled.

"It looks to me like these motherfuckers just got jacked for some unknown quantity of drug-dealer, human-trafficking money."

"We can't take that," Drew said

"Oh yes you can, that is unless you want to stay around and explain what you all were doing out here in the middle of fucking nowhere with a bunch of dead bodies."

No one said a word as the thought of the investigation sank in.

"Look," Ramirez said, "the way I see it, me and your friend Gerardo here are fucking heroes. The feds have been after this dude for a few years, there's even a hefty reward. I will tell them how Gerardo here saved my life and saved these kids. He gets witness protection and status here in the United States. Maybe he even gets the reward money. The last thing that Border Protection and ICE want is for the public to know about another dirty agent's involvement in the trafficking of children for pedophiles. No one is going to believe anything this *narco* piece of shit," Ramirez gestured back to the truck and Caritas, "has to say, and you can believe that he is looking at a hefty federal prison sentence."

Drew walked over to the truck and started going through Caritas' pockets. He pulled the wallet out of Caritas' back pocket and found Caritas' cellphone in his front pocket.

"Well," Drew said as he pulled the driver's licenses of each of them from the wallet, "we don't want anyone finding these."

Drew dropped the phone on the ground and crushed it with three stomps from the heel of his boot.

He reached down and brushed through the debris and picked up the SIM card.

"Just making sure that they won't find anything with our info on it."

"You saved my life and these kids' lives," Ramirez said, passion written on his face. "I can never repay you, but at the very least you can believe that I will never tell anyone about you guys."

Drew nodded. "What now?"

"Now," Ramirez said looking out over the scene, "we wipe down the guns and the vehicles. You take the truck. I will wait with your buddy here for an hour before I call this in. That should give you enough time to get back to your cars and ditch the truck."

"And then?" Chino asked.

"And then you guys are gone like the wind. You never existed."

Drew and Chino worked their way through the truck and trailer, wiping down surfaces they may have touched and then went back over all the surfaces and wiped them down again. They finished and walked over to the truck where Gerardo, Ramirez, and Chance were gathered.

"I think we're done here," Drew said.

Chino stepped forward and extended his hand for Gerardo to shake.

"Thanks, man," he said. "We might all be dead without you."

"I think we all would have been dead without each other," he said.

"Good luck, amigo," Drew said to Gerardo as he shook his hand.

"A word of caution, amigos," Gerardo said in a somber tone, "I know these types of people. They have extended family and are very attached to their money and pride. Lay low for a while."

"I don't think any of us is going to buy a Hummer anytime soon," Drew said with a laugh.

Chance used the front of his shirt to wipe some of the dried blood off his face.

"You guys ever thought of opening up a bar?" he asked.

Chino and Drew did not say anything.

"A small bar, just a place where we could all work and make some safe money."

"I think I know a couple of dudes with a little bit of money to invest," Drew said with a tired smile.

"I think I know what you *cabrones* can call it," Gerardo said.

"And what would that be?" Chance asked.

"I kind of like 'Gordo's Last Stand.'"

Chance let out a pained laugh through his swollen mouth. All five men stood for a few long seconds saying nothing. Then after a nod from Drew, they turned and walked back to the truck.

***

It was late Saturday morning when Drew drove up the driveway to his house. He had never been so happy to be in one place until that moment. He stayed in his truck for a minute after he turned off the ignition. He stretched back in his seat and with a few deep breaths tried to exhale all the danger and death from the night before. He couldn't help but replay the evening in his head, the bad things that happened and the worse that could have happened. Just then he saw a tiny hand pull back the curtain in the living room window. Little Drew's face popped into view. He was beaming a smile that seemed to take up his entire face. He waved.

Drew waved back and began to cry.

EPILOGUE
CHRONICLE NEWS SERVICE
Jan. 4, 2019

Feds probe Border Patrol connection to child-trafficking ring

Border Patrol agents may have been involved with a ring that smuggled children into the United States from Mexico so they could be sold to sex offenders.

The FBI has launched a wide-ranging investigation of agents' ties to the ring, which is associated with a narcotics cartel based in the Mexican state of Sinaloa, federal sources confirmed. The sources spoke on the condition that they remain anonymous because they don't have permission to speak publicly about the probe.

Children were traded and sold in an established network of sex offenders that extended to 22 states, the sources said. Vincent Corriente-Torres, known as "Caritas," is suspected of leading the ring that sold children to pedophiles, the sources said.

Corriente-Torres holds dual citizenship in Mexico and the United States, and he is a graduate of La Jolla High School. His uncle is cartel kingpin Hector Torres-Reyes, known as "Cicatriz" (Scar), who has been indicted in the United States on drug-trafficking and murder charges.

Corriente-Torres is in federal custody, the sources said, but they would not say where he is being held.

They also would not comment on whether the child-trafficking ring is connected to an incident in June of last year near Boulevard in which two Border Patrol agents were shot to death in a ranch house.

Federal officials have released few details about what happened in the house, other than to say the men were killed while attempting to apprehend human traffickers.

Border Patrol, Customs and Border Protection and Immigration and Customs Enforcement officials declined to comment.

DON'T MISS THE SEQUEL TO THE
SILENCE AND THE DARK COMING
FROM MARC CARLOS AND
MOONSHINE COVE IN 2020:

THE SILENCE AND THE DEATH

The first chapter begins on the next
page.

ONE

He ran. He didn't think. He didn't look back. He just ran. He increased his foot turnover to ramp up his speed. He had trained for this. The trick was not to go into an all-out sprint but to control your gait and breathing while increasing your speed. He never knew where or on what type of surface he would have to run, but he knew one day he would have to run. For his life. He always wore soft, rubber-soled tactical boots in case he had to do just this. Run. The adrenaline kicked in, and he felt as if he was moving faster than he ever had. In a way, it was cathartic. He heard nothing except the sound of his breathing. His feet bounced off the pavement, each step propelling him farther.

He came home from work. The normal slow climb up the exterior stairwell to his apartment. But before he reached the top step, he saw the front door to his apartment was slightly ajar. He knew he shut the door and locked it, just like he did every time he left. The small, white, folded piece of paper he wedged into the jamb was now lying on the mat in front of the door. No, he was not mistaken. Someone was inside. Waiting.

He stopped dead. For a second, he couldn't move. He couldn't breathe. He began to back slowly down the steps as quietly as he could. Retracing his path as if backing out of a minefield. He kept his eyes trained on the door.

When he reached ground level, he stopped. Still no movement above him in the apartment. He looked out to the street. Normal, residential. Nothing out of the ordinary. The apartment complex across the street had a few people milling about, but no one looking over at him. Maybe he overreacted. Maybe he left and forgot to shut the door completely.

Then he saw it.

The vinyl blinds were drawn as usual, but for a brief second, he saw one of the slats move. Someone was looking out.

He turned and ran.

Witness protection, he thought, *puta madre!*

He knew they could never truly protect him, so he was always ready to run. What were the chances that Cicatriz, the Sinaloa Cartel, or any of the other assorted low-life criminals that he had wronged would not come looking for him? He remembered one of the last things that Caritas had taunted him with.

"We know who you are, *Detective!*"

Gerardo had no reason to doubt him.

How far had he run now, half mile? Mile? He didn't know. What mattered was that he didn't hear the ping of bullets or the roar of car engines. Still, here he was running like a crazy man down an orange-tree-lined road in Riverside. Maybe not such a good idea for a Latino to be sprinting fully clothed on a Southern California street with a bunch of trigger-happy police on patrol.

The hot August night, with the daytime heat and humidity still hanging low against the pavement, stuck to his body. Every breath seemed to be a swallow of hot steam. He spotted an orange grove to his right about a hundred meters away. He had passed the set of groves connected to UC Riverside on countless occasions on his way to work. The grove extended off the road for a few dark blocks. That had to be his play. He increased his speed and did not look back. He knew every foot of distance he put between himself and whoever was chasing him could save his life. His heart was screaming out of his chest, but he pushed past the pain. He came up alongside the grove and saw an opening in the wire fencing. He cut hard and veered into the grove. The moment his feet hit the grove soil his pace slowed. The dirt was loose and thick. The smell of a recent watering permeated the air. Gerardo zigzagged to a dark place in the grove's center. He dropped to the ground. He leaned his back against a large orange tree, his heart pounding, his lungs gasping for oxygen. He tried to moderate the citrus- and earth-tinged air. What was it that the Marine told him? Deep breath, focus on controlling your heart rate.

He remembered back to that night in the desert. He knew then his involvement in rescuing the children would haunt him, but he had plenty of other things that kept him up at night. He dropped to his stomach to get a better view of the street. The moist soil had a healthy, fertile smell. As his hands dug into the dirt, he remembered his neighbor telling him that the groves had been here over a hundred years. One hundred years of Mexicans like him tending this rich, black soil. Still, here he was running for his life, lying face down in the dirt. It was still dirt. He could never escape it.

He stayed still, his dark clothing melting into the night. He could see the roadway about one hundred yards away. Cars passed by sporadically, the drivers oblivious to the execution awaiting the man in the grove. Then he saw a vehicle slow to a stop. It was a Suburban or some other equally oversized vehicle. The doors opened, and three men got out of the vehicle. Gerardo was far enough away that he could not make out any facial features. He had no doubt they were here to kill him. One of the men turned on a flashlight. The powerful beam traversed the grove. Gerardo lowered his head into the earth and pressed hard. The dirt entered the side of his mouth as

225

he kept his head turned to get a partial view. The beam passed right over him. His heart started pounding faster. Breathe. Deep cleansing breath. Like the Marine had told him. He debated whether to get up and run. He had a good hundred yards head start. They, on the other hand, had guns and an SUV. This was an urban place not farmland, despite the old stand of citrus he found. Once he left the grove, he would be exposed. He decided to wait. What was the worst that could happen? Two bullets in the back of the head out here in the dirt where he deserved to die?

Just then, with his head still pressed against the dirt, he heard the doors of the vehicle shut and the engine start. He didn't lift his head or move for a solid three minutes. A single ant casually crawled across his face, but he could not move to knock it away. When he lifted his head, he saw the SUV was gone. Still, he remained faced down in the dirt and darkness another thirty minutes before he lifted himself to lean against the tree. During that time, Gerardo had time to think about his past, his decision to get involved with those men in the desert, and whether this would truly ever end.

Gerardo took one more long look around the grove for signs of the men or the vehicle. When he was certain he was alone, he reached into his front pocket and pulled out his phone. He looked one more time toward the road to make sure his eyes had not deceived him. He pulled the phone up close to his chest and turned it on. The glow from the phone lit up his face. If there were anyone out there, they would certainly be able to see the light beacon he had created. With the phone powered up, he opened his contacts. When he found the numbers he was looking for, he began to text.

He typed one word. ALAMO. Gerardo looked out at the dark expanse of orange trees and hit SEND.

CPSIA information can be obtained
at www.ICGtesting.com
Printed in the USA
BVHW071546201220
595951BV00003B/193